DOCTOR WHO

Touched by an Angel

JONATHAN MORRIS

BBC
BOOKS

9 10 8

Published in 2011 by BBC Books, an imprint of Ebury Publishing.
A Random House Group Company

Doctor Who is a BBC Wales production for BBC One.
Executive producers: Steven Moffat, Piers Wenger and Beth Willis

The Random House Group Limited Reg. No. 954009

Addresses for companies within the Random House Group can be found at www.randomhouse.co.uk

A CIP catalogue record for this book is available from the British Library

ISBN 978 1 849 90234 2

The Random House Group Limited supports The Forest Stewardship Council® (FSC®), the leading international forest-certification organisation. Our books carrying the FSC label are printed on FSC®-certified paper. FSC is the only forest-certification scheme supported by the leading environmental organisations, including Greenpeace. Our paper procurement policy can be found at www.randomhouse.co.uk/environment

Commissioning editor: Albert DePetrillo
Editorial manager: Nicholas Payne
Series consultant: Justin Richards
Project editor: Steve Tribe
Cover design: Lee Binding © Woodlands Books Ltd, 2011
Production: Rebecca Jones

Printed and bound in Great Britain by Clays Ltd, St Ives PLC

To buy books by your favourite authors and register for offers, visit www.randomhouse.co.uk

To my wife, Debbie

10 April 2003

Slosh-thwack! Slosh-thwack! Slosh-thwack!

The rain splattered against the windscreen before the wipers swiped the glass clean, patting the water down into a splashy trough above the dashboard. Beyond, the car headlights picked out the narrow country lane rolling out of the darkness, the high hedges on either side giving it the feel of driving through a tunnel.

Rebecca rubbed her forehead. Another headache. Probably due to the idiot who had spent the last five miles behind her, his headlights blazing away in her rear-view mirror. Or exhaustion from driving non-stop from London. There was definitely no other reason for her headache. OK, so she'd been having them almost daily since the accident, but that was no reason to go and see a doctor, no matter what Mark said.

Rebecca felt a flush of anger. Mark should be with her now, paying the traditional bi-monthly visit to her parents in Chilbury. He had an excuse, of course; he always had an excuse. There was a crisis at work and he had volunteered to work late to sort it out, as usual.

Slosh-thwack! Slosh-thwack! Slosh-thwack!

The radio hissed as it lost the signal for *The World Tonight*. It didn't matter, Rebecca already knew what the news would be. It would be all about the invasion of Iraq. The television news had been full of nothing else for weeks; journalists in flak jackets reporting live from hotel rooms, interspersed with infra-red footage of green blobs flashing back and forth over a burning city. It was like watching someone commentating on a computer game.

Today's big story had been about American soldiers pulling down a statue of Saddam Hussein in some dusty town square while the reporter burbled excitedly about it being a momentous event in history. Seeing the footage of the conquering heroes draping their flag over the fallen statue, Rebecca had felt sick and ashamed. They'd be handing out chocolate bars next.

Slosh-thwack! Slosh-thwack! Slosh-thwack!

Rebecca twisted the dial for Radio 1. A plaintive piano riff emerged from the speakers, introducing *Beautiful* by Christina Aguilera. Rebecca left the song playing; it suited her mood and wouldn't distract her from driving.

Slosh-thwack! Slosh-thwack! Slosh-thwack!

Approaching a sharp left turn, Rebecca changed down to second gear. She turned the corner, to be suddenly confronted by two brilliant shining lights bearing down upon her.

A horn blared out like a monster's roar. Instinctively Rebecca wrenched the steering wheel to the left to avoid the oncoming heavy goods lorry. The left-hand side of her car went into the hedge, leaves and brambles scraping along the side. Her heart pounding, Rebecca remembered, too late, to apply the brakes.

The front of her car smashed into the grille of the lorry and the windscreen shattered into a million beads of glass. The impact threw Rebecca forward, her seatbelt tightening so much it crushed the wind out of her lungs. Barely a second later, Rebecca found herself being thrown to the side as her car rolled over. Rebecca had a brief sense memory of being on a theme park roller-coaster ride. She had never liked roller-coaster rides.

Her only other thought was to observe with wry amusement that this was like something out of *Casualty*.

The next thing she knew, she was lying in her seat, gazing across a muddy field. Lying in her seat? Her seat had been upturned and her weight rested on her back. But if she was still inside the car, why could she feel the rain upon her face? She couldn't feel any pain, though, which was a relief.

Rebecca cursed herself. How many times had her mother moaned on the telephone about lorries using the village as a shortcut, even though the council had installed speed cameras? It was an accident waiting to happen, she'd said. Turned out she'd been right.

Rebecca wondered why everything in the field had an orange hue, as though lit by a street lamp. A second later, everything went dark, before lighting up again with the same orange hue. The lorry must have activated its warning lights. What had happened to the lorry driver? For a moment, Rebecca hoped that he'd been hurt, it would serve him right, before banishing the thought. She'd been very lucky not to be injured.

But if she was OK, why couldn't she move? Rebecca tried wriggling in her seat; her seatbelt was so tight she could hardly breathe. But nothing happened. She wanted to wipe the rain out of her eyes, but for some reason her hands didn't respond. She began to wonder whether she might've been hurt after all.

Outside the car, the orange light blinked back on.

Now that was weird. About six metres away, in the field, stood a statue, like might be found in a graveyard or a Roman museum. The statue was of a young woman with coiled hair wearing a flowing robe. It had two wings. An angel. The statue stood hunched, burying its head in its hands as though crying. To add to the effect, rain trickled from between its fingers.

The light blinked off, returning Rebecca to blackness. She thought briefly of bonfires, of Guy Fawkes Night and toffee apples. Why was she thinking about bonfires? And then she realised she could smell burning.

The orange light blinked on again. Rebecca couldn't be sure, but hadn't the statue of the angel been holding its head in its hands? Because now it was looking towards her with blank, pupil-less eyes.

There was darkness again. Then orange light.

The statue had moved closer now. Still staring at her with its impassive, stony eyes. Its mouth was now slightly open, as though drawing in breath to speak.

Darkness. Orange light.

It now stood only two metres away. It filled her view, looming over her.

Caught in the flickering glow of a fire, thick black smoke billowing around it, its expression had changed to a snarl of hunger. Its lips had drawn back to reveal rows of sharp fangs, like those of a bat. It reached towards her with outstretched hands, its long fingernails like talons.

But this was impossible, Rebecca thought. It wasn't moving. *It wasn't moving.*

Chapter 1

7 October 2011

Toby Murray was a difficult man to like. He had a pudgy, red face, he was flabby and sweaty, and he affected a very bad East End accent.

'We wanna win this one, Mark. We wanna take 'em dahn.'

Mark sighed. This wasn't *Law & Order*, this was a routine piece of contract law. He'd only taken it on because Toby's employers were one of Pollard, Boyce & Whitaker's most prestigious clients, and because Toby had, rather pathetically, insisted on dealing with a senior partner. But if Toby wanted to be fed a load of high-powered gibberish, Mark would be only too happy to provide.

'Nevertheless, I recommend we pick our battles carefully,' said Mark. 'Find as many areas of common ground as we can, because at the moment our position is about as solid as a soufflé.'

'So, what you saying? What's our next move?'

'Make an audit of every contract, all the ones that have been fulfilled, all the ones that haven't. I need points of contact, dates, emails and paper trails, everything you can give me.'

Toby nodded and stood up. 'You'll have it next Monday.'

Mark pressed the button to summon his personal assistant. 'Take as long as it takes.'

Toby glanced around the room, his eyes resting on the photograph that Mark kept on the shelf opposite his desk. Toby whistled in admiration as he picked up the photograph. 'Who's the babe?'

The photograph showed Rebecca perched on the balcony of their hotel room in Rome. The morning sun shone in her hair like a halo and gave her skin a golden glow. Her eyes were wide and impossibly blue and a contented smile curled across her lips.

'My, ah, wife,' said Mark, feeling a sudden flush of anger. 'If you could just put that back...'

'The missus? Bit young, ain't she? Well done!'

'It was taken a while ago, if you could just put it back—'

'Oh, got you.' Toby returned the photograph to the shelf. 'Former glories. Mine's the same. Second you stick a ring on their finger, they start to inflate. It's like there's a valve.'

Siobhan appeared in the doorway. 'All done, Mr Whitaker?'

'I think so,' said Mark curtly. 'Mr Murray has important business to attend to, no doubt.'

Mark offered his hand to Toby. Toby clasped it and

attempted to crush Mark's fingers. Toby was one of those men who felt it important to establish he was the Alpha Male.

'Laters, mate,' said Toby, releasing him.

Siobhan guided Toby out of the office before returning and closing the door so they wouldn't be disturbed. 'Are you all right?'

'What?' said Mark, rubbing some feeling back into his fingers.

'Only I heard you mention your wife.'

'Oh. Toby was just checking out the photo of her, that's all.'

'I see,' said Siobhan. Siobhan was an attractive, dark-skinned woman in her forties, a lethal combination of a gentle smile and a no-nonsense attitude. She studied the photograph of Rebecca. 'She looks very happy.'

'She was,' said Mark proudly. 'That was taken the morning after we first got together.'

Siobhan turned to give Mark a concerned look. 'How long has it been now, since the accident? Eight years?'

'Yes,' said Mark, avoiding her gaze by glancing out of his window at the rush-hour traffic on the Croydon flyover. Grey clouds filled the gloomy sky. It got dark so quickly these days.

'Eight years. That's a long time for you to still be torturing yourself. Rebecca wouldn't want that.'

'You don't know what Rebecca would want.'

'She'd want you to be happy. Rather than using what happened as an excuse to be miserable.'

'An excuse?'

'You should get out more. Meet new people.

Women. Single, *alive* women.'

'Is this about Charlotte?' Two weeks ago, Mark had gone on a date with Siobhan's friend Charlotte, an attractive, friendly woman whose idea of a good night out sadly did not extend to spending three hours in a wine bar listening to her date talk about his dead wife.

'Not necessarily,' said Siobhan. 'I have other friends. There's Susannah, Joanne—'

'Thanks, but no thanks. Was there anything else?'

'Only this.' Siobhan slid a battered, padded envelope about the size of a paperback across his desk. Mark picked it up. His name and today's date were scrawled on the front: *MARK WHITAKER. 7/10/2011.*

'Has this just come in?' said Mark, turning over the envelope.

'No. Bit weird, actually. Apparently it's been gathering dust in the archive for the last eight years, with strict instructions that it should be delivered to you on this date.'

'Eight years?'

'A mystery package, eh? Well, are you gonna open it?'

Mark ran a finger over the flap where the envelope had been stapled shut. Something about this envelope made him uneasy. His back suddenly felt as cold as a gravestone. 'No,' he said. 'If it's waited eight years, a few more hours won't hurt.'

Then he realised what was odd about the envelope. The name on the front was written *in his own handwriting*.

It had gone eight by the time he made his way down

to reception. If anybody else had stayed behind in the office, they'd have thought he was working late, when in fact he'd spent the last hour playing Killer Sudokus on the computer. Putting off the moment when he'd have to step out into the wind and the rain and begin the drive back to his cold, empty flat.

'Night, Mr Whitaker, sir,' said Ron, the overnight security guard.

Mark nodded to avoid engaging Ron in conversation, because he would have to ask about Ron's children and he couldn't for the life of him remember their names.

'Lovely weather, eh?' said Ron, indicating the street outside. The windows and glass doors had misted up, making the street lights look like smudges in the darkness.

'Yeah, well, goodnight, Ron,' said Mark. But before he turned to go he glanced at the closed-circuit television on Ron's desk. Something had caught his eye. The black-and-white screen showed the reception area, facing out towards the street. Where someone stood peering in through one of the doors, their face almost touching the glass. As though waiting to come in. Mark turned to look at the door, but there was nobody there. He turned back to the monitor on Ron's desk, but it had flicked over to show a view of one of the office stairwells. When it flicked back to the view of the reception area, there was no longer a face at the door.

Ron paused as he turned the page of his *Daily Mirror*. 'Was there something, sir?'

'No, no, nothing.' Mark buttoned up his coat and headed out into the night, taking care to use a different door from the one in which he had seen the marble-white, staring face.

The rain eased off to a drizzle as Mark pulled into the petrol station. Pulling his coat tightly around him, he stepped into the freezing night and glugged thirty pounds of unleaded into the tank. He started to walk towards the shop to pay when he remembered the envelope, which he'd placed on the passenger seat. For all he knew, it might contain confidential legal documents and was not the sort of thing he should leave unattended.

Mark returned to his car and studied the envelope under the forecourt light. The name on the front definitely looked like his handwriting, but that didn't mean anything; someone else could have similar handwriting to him. But he was intrigued as to why anyone would leave an envelope with instructions for it to only be delivered eight years later. And why *7/10/2011*? What was so important about that date? Mark poked a finger under the flap and tore it open, just enough to see inside.

The envelope contained at least a hundred neatly folded fifty-pound notes, with several sheets of paper wrapped around them.

Siobhan had been right, it was a real mystery. But it would have to wait. Mark stowed the envelope into his coat pocket, locked his car and made his way into the shop.

It was one of those petrol station stops that was like a small supermarket, selling newspapers, magazines and microwaved sausage rolls. There were no other customers. Mark hurried to the counter to be served by a young Asian who didn't look up from his smartphone. 'Thirty quid.'

Mark slotted his card into the chip-and-pin and typed in his number. As he waited for the machine to respond, he glanced over the attendant's shoulder at a monitor showing the output of the petrol station's closed-circuit cameras. The screen showed a view from a point above the counter, looking down into the shop. Mark could see the attendant and himself at the counter in grainy, flickering black-and-white. And behind him, at the end of the aisle near the door, stood a statue of an angel.

That was ridiculous. If there'd been a statue by the door, he'd have noticed it on his way in. Mark frowned at the picture on the screen. It was an old statue, its surface crumbling and pitted. It stood hunched, holding its face in its hands.

Mark turned to look back down the aisle. It was empty. Where the statue had stood – where the statue should've been standing – there was just shiny, wet floor.

Mark returned his gaze to the monitor and shuddered. The statue was still there, at the end of the aisle. But hadn't it been standing further away? And hadn't it been holding its head in its hands? Because now it seemed to have moved a metre or so towards him, and had lowered its hands, cupping them as though in prayer.

He turned to look back down the aisle once more. It was still empty. No statue, nothing.

He looked back at the monitor. The statue had moved

again. It was looking up, directly into the camera lens. Looking at him. With staring, blank eyes and a slightly parted mouth. And a couple of metres in front of it he could see himself, standing at the counter, looking up at the monitor, and the attendant, still tapping away on his smartphone.

The PIN machine beeped and the attendant tore off Mark's receipt. Mark mumbled some thanks and turned to go. Thankfully, the shop was still empty. His heart thudding, Mark hurried out of the shop, taking care to avoid the aisle where the statue had been standing.

He sprinted back to the safety of his car and slammed the door shut. He was just overtired, that was it. That was the only possible explanation.

It was with some apprehension that Mark checked the car's rear-view mirror. But there was nothing there, nothing sitting on the passenger seat behind him, nothing standing in the forecourt. He was alone.

After parking near his flat in Bromley, Mark headed to the high street to get some dinner. Huddling himself into his coat, he trudged down the road, his eyes fixed on the pavement to avoid the puddles. An ambulance siren whined in the distance, but apart from that, he could have been the only man alive on the planet.

Mark hurried on to the Taste Of The Orient. Inside it was dry and warm and smelt of sizzled rice. A couple of kids sat waiting by the window, chatting. A petite Chinese girl emerged from the kitchen and took Mark's order: sweet-and-sour pork, egg-fried rice. Mark paid her with the last ten-pound note in his wallet.

Mark glanced around for something to occupy his

attention. Mounted on the wall behind the counter a monitor showed the output of a closed-circuit camera. It showed the entrance of the Chinese restaurant, it showed the couple by the window, and it showed Mark.

And standing right behind him, there was the statue of the angel, the same one from the petrol station. But now it was reaching towards Mark's back with an outstretched bare arm.

Mark felt an icy shiver and, holding his breath, turned to look behind him. There was nothing there, just the rain-streaked window of the takeaway.

He turned to look back up at the monitor. The statue had taken another step closer. It was still reaching towards him. On the screen, Mark could see the coils carved for the angel's hair, the feathers in its wings and its unseeing, blank eyes. And he could see himself at the counter, looking up at the monitor. The statue's fingers were almost brushing the back of his neck.

Choking with terror, Mark lunged towards the door of the Chinese takeaway, shoved it open and stumbled into the darkness, the icy wind biting his face. Not daring to look back, he ran down the high street, running so fast his stomach ached.

He had to get home. He would be safe there, safe from… safe from whatever this thing was.

Mark slowed to a jog, his heart thumping in protest, and continued down the high street. Past the bookmaker's. Past the Halal butchers. Past the hi-fi shop—

Suddenly all the televisions in the shop window flickered into life. It had a video camera as part of the window display, a camera that was now pointing at Mark. He could see himself on the screens; the same image repeated, over and over again, of him staring into the window.

The statue was right behind him, reaching for his neck, its mouth open to reveal hideous jagged teeth.

'Don't look back. Don't turn around, don't close your eyes, and whatever you do, *don't look back!*'

The voice came from behind Mark. It sounded like the voice of a young man but with the authority of someone much older.

'What?' said Mark, frozen to the spot.

'Keep your eyes on the screen! It's vitally important you don't let it touch you.'

'And how do I do that?'

'It's quantum-locked. It can only move if somebody isn't looking at it.'

'Quantum-locked?'

'You know, the Heisenberg uncertainty principle, the very act of observation affects the nature of the object being observed. Amy, Rory. Keep watching the screens. Take turns blinking.'

'Righty-ho,' said a girl with a Scottish accent from behind Mark's left ear.

'Watch the televisions, got you, no problem,' said a young man nervously.

'And try not to blink at the same time,' said the voice of authority. 'That would be utterly disastrous. *Good*. Now, bloke-watching-himself-on-the-television, move forward. Very slowly.'

Mark swallowed and stepped forward until his nose was nearly touching the shop window.

'Good. Now take two steps to your right. *Slowly!*'

Mark took two steps to the right, watching himself on the television screens as he edged out of reach of the angel. 'What is that thing?'

'It's a kind of... temporal scavenger. Or a predator. One of the two. Or both.'

'Rory, I'm going to blink... *now!*' said the Scottish girl.

'But it's made of stone,' said Mark.

'Defence mechanism,' said the voice of authority. 'You see, you can't kill a stone.'

'Can't you?'

'Well, nobody's attempted it and lived.'

'Amy, I'm gonna blink... *now!*' said the nervous young man.

'OK, it's safe to look back now,' said the voice of authority.

Taking a deep breath, Mark turned around, to see a tall, pretty girl with long, fiery hair and a young man with a prominent nose and a woolly chullo hat, both staring attentively at the window. Beside them stood a handsome young man with angular cheekbones and thick brown hair swept up into a fringe. With his tweed jacket and bow tie, he looked like he was on his way to a fancy dress party as Albert Einstein.

There was no sign of the statue. 'But there... there's nothing here!' stammered Mark.

'No.' The man in the tweed jacket had a device like an old-fashioned tape recorder slung over one shoulder and he twirled a stubby, torch-like device in his hand like a pop star performing a trick with a microphone. He levelled the device at the window and it emitted a high-pitched drone and glowed green. 'No, this *particular* Weeping Angel has no corporeal form.'

'What does that mean?'

'It means it only exists within the televisions. Within *every* television. That which holds the image of an Angel becomes, itself, an Angel.'

'So it can't come out of the screen and get us?' said the girl with red hair. 'Rory, I'm going to blink... *now!*'

'No, don't think so. It must be very weak, running on fumes.'

'But it can still touch me?' said Mark.

'If you're being looked at by a camera, yes. It's on the screen, your image is on the screen, so it can make contact with your image, and thus... you.'

'Amy, I'm gonna blink... *now!*' said the man with the prominent nose.

'Who are you?' said Mark. 'And how do you know so much about these things?'

'I'm the man who's going to save your life. You can call me *the Doctor*.'

'The Doctor?'

'And in answer to your second question, I've met the Weeping Angels before. I detected this one using *this*.' The Doctor indicated the old-fashioned tape recorder. 'Whenever the space-time continuum goes wibbly, it lights up.' The Doctor tapped the recorder in frustration. 'Or it would do if the bulb worked. It also boils eggs. That's not a fault, it's a feature.'

'Rory, I'm going to blink... *now!*'

'Strange thing is, the Angel isn't the source of the wibbliness,' said the Doctor. 'No. It's *you*.'

'Me?'

The Doctor peered at Mark. 'It must've chosen you for a *reason*. I wonder *why*? What's so great about you?'

'Nothing,' said Mark. 'So what you're saying is, that thing's after me, and you don't know why?'

'No. Haven't the slightest idea!'

'But if it can't be killed... how do I get away from it?'

'You can't.'

'But if I run—'

'This whole street is covered by security cameras. You'd never make it.'

'Rory, shouldn't you be telling me it's my turn to blink now?' said Amy.

'What? Oh,' gulped Rory. 'Sorry, um, I thought it was my turn...'

And then Mark realised that Amy and Rory were looking at each other and not the window.

Mark turned. On all the televisions, he could see himself, the Doctor, Rory and Amy – and the Angel, frozen as it lunged towards his back, its face contorted into a grimace of rage. Another second and it would've made contact.

Panic took over. Mark stumbled backwards, turning away from the Angel, and broke into a run. He heard the Doctor and his friends shouting after him, but it was no good. He had to get away.

He'd made it. He'd actually made it. He could see the block of flats where he lived, the front doorway bathed in the glow of an electric light.

Mark gasped for breath. He'd sprinted down the high street, feeling suddenly and terribly conscious of every security camera. They were everywhere, mounted high on walls and lamp posts, all staring downwards with unblinking glass eyes. To avoid being caught, he'd taken a long route home to avoid garages and illuminated shops. He'd even hidden from a passing double-decker bus. They had cameras on buses now, didn't they?

But he was OK. Cold and wet, but OK. Mark hurried up the concrete steps to the entrance, past the garden and the recycling bins, until at last he reached the door. He dug out his keys from his coat, found the one for the door, and slid it in the lock. And then he realised.

There was a camera looking directly at him. The camera of the door's videophone.

Something as cold as marble touched the back of his neck.

For a split second, Mark could see his horrified reflection, and that of the Angel behind him, its hand on his neck, its jaws wide open and its tongue extended, as though about to bite.

And then he was gone.

Chapter 2

Rory and Amy struggled to keep up with the Doctor as he dashed through the gloomy, rain-soaked backstreets, his wibble-detector held in front of him. 'This way! Hurry!'

Rory had no idea where they were. They'd been running through identical housing estates for fifteen minutes and he'd lost all sense of direction.

'Here!' The Doctor halted, circled on the spot, and indicated a block of flats set back from the road. They looked perfectly ordinary to Rory, except that by the entrance he could see the statue of an Angel, its body hunched, holding its face in its hands.

'What's happened?' asked Rory. 'Something bad, right?'

'Quiet.' The Doctor advanced on the statue like a naturalist creeping up on a sleeping lion. Calmly and steadily, he made his way up the steps towards it.

'Careful!' whispered Amy.

The Doctor gave her a thank-you-for-stating-the-obvious stare, then stooped to examine the Angel. It didn't move. He buzzed it experimentally with his sonic screwdriver and tried covering his own eyes, as though playing peek-a-boo, but nothing happened. The Doctor tapped it on the wing. A chunk of it crumbled to dust under his fingers. 'It's safe, I think.'

'How safe?' said Amy.

'As safe as a doornail.'

'But I thought you said these things fed on, what was it, potential time energy?' said Rory as he followed Amy to the Doctor's side.

'All the life left unlived,' muttered the Doctor. 'Normally, they zap people back in time, whoosh, that's how they get their five-a-day.'

'Normally?'

'Whereas in this case, this Angel *used up* its last reserves of energy to send its victim into the past. Sacrificing itself, like a bee dying after its sting. But not like a bee at all. No, now it's more like a garden ornament.' As the Doctor spoke, one of the Angel's arms broke off, followed by both the wings, before the Angel toppled forward, smashing itself to pieces with a heavy crash.

'But why do that?' asked Amy, regarding the debris warily. 'Why kill itself rather than feed?'

'Maybe it couldn't.' The Doctor dusted down his jacket and trousers. 'Or maybe this is a new type of Weeping Angel.'

'You mean they come in different varieties now? Oh, *great!*'

'It must've been drawn to its prey… like a moth to a flame.' The Doctor's eyes widened in delight. 'Hang on! That analogy made sense. My analogies *never* make sense. I must write it down. Rory, write it down for me!'

'I'm not your secretary, Doctor,' said Rory patiently.

'No? Only there *is* a vacancy, yours if you want it.'

Rory spotted a set of keys hanging from the lock of the door and took them for safe keeping. 'Shouldn't we be more worried about the guy it zapped? Find out where he is?'

'Not really a question of *where*,' smiled the Doctor. 'More a question of *when*.' He adjusted his wibble-detector. 'Yes! A residual time trace. Fading fast but we *should* be able to follow it. Come on!'

'Shouldn't we find out who he is first?' said Rory. 'We don't even know his name.' He jangled the keys in his hand.

'What do you suggest?' snapped the Doctor in exasperation. 'We try those keys in every door in the building until we find out which flat belongs to him?'

'Yes.'

'There isn't time.'

'I could do it, while you go off and do your time-trace thing. And then, once you know where – and when – he is, you can pop back here and pick me up.'

'That's a *terrible* idea.' The Doctor paused, lost in thought, then grinned. 'No, actually, that's an *excellent* idea. You're OK with that?'

'You know me, Doctor, anything to help.'

'I do know you, that is *absolutely* correct, but nevertheless you remain disconcertingly full of surprises. Very good. I'll be back here in exactly one hour. Come on, Pond. We have a time trace to follow!'

Amy gave Rory a sympathetic smile and a squeeze, then set off after the Doctor.

The statue had vanished. One second it had been touching his neck. The next, it wasn't there.

Mark sighed with relief and reached down to turn the door key, only to find that had also disappeared. He checked, but his keys hadn't fallen to the ground.

Looking around, Mark noticed that it had stopped raining. In fact, the pavement and roads were completely dry. The sky, rather than being dark and overcast, had become a clear, early-evening blue, with a full moon.

Mark checked his pockets. Still no keys. Oh well, he'd given a spare to Mrs Levenson in Flat 12. Mark rang her doorbell.

'Yes?' replied a young female voice through the crackle.

'It's Mark.'

'Mark?'

'I've locked myself out. Can you buzz me in please?'

'Did you say Mark?'

'Yes. From next door?'

'No Mark next door.'

'Mrs Levenson, it's me, you can see me on the video thing.'

'You have wrong flat. No Mrs Levenson here.'

The intercom went dead. Mark swore under his breath and, taking care he'd got the right one, pressed the *12* button again.

'Go away please, you have wrong flat.' The woman had a Spanish accent, or something close to it.

'I live in number 11. Mark Whitaker. I don't know who you are, but—'

'No Mark Whitaker in number 11. Number 11 Mr and Mrs Ramprakash.'

'Look, can I speak to Mrs Levenson, please?'

'I told you. No Mrs Levenson here. Go away now, please, or I will call police.'

The intercom went dead. Mark considered trying another flat but no one else would have a key. He'd have to call Mrs Levenson on his mobile. Which he'd left in his car.

With a growing sense of unease, Mark set off for the street where he'd parked. As he walked, he heard the sound of birds chirruping. Like on a warm summer evening.

Rory tried the key in the door of number 12 and gave it a jiggle. Nope. He moved quietly on as a burst of studio audience laughter came from the other side of the door.

Number 11. Jiggle. The door swung open to reveal a hallway. Some envelopes slithered on the doormat. Rory stooped to pick them up.

'Hello, can I help you?'

'Wh-what?' Rory gave a guilty gasp. An extremely short, round, elderly woman stood in the doorway of number 12. She glared at him through thick, pink-rimmed glasses.

'Hi, er, yes,' said Rory. 'I'm a friend of the, um, bloke who lives here.'

The woman regarded him suspiciously. 'A *friend*?'

'Yeah. From work. He asked me to pop in and get a... thing.'

'Mr Whitaker doesn't have friends.'

'Doesn't he? Right. And you call him Mr Whitaker.' Rory glanced at the front of one of the envelopes. 'Mark Whitaker. Marky. The Markster. The Markulator.' Rory straightened up. 'You might be able to do me a favour, actually. Only we're a bit concerned about Mark at work. We think he might be in some kind of trouble, but you know old Mark, plays his cards close to his chest. So, if he's mentioned anything, anything at all?'

The woman stared at Rory, sizing him up. 'You're a friend from work?'

'Look, he'd hardly give me his key and ask me to pop into his flat to get him a... thing if we didn't know each other, would he?' Rory gave her the same reassuring smile he reserved for elderly patients at Leadworth hospital. 'I tell you what. Why don't you come in with me? I'll make you a nice cup of tea, we'll have a sit down and a bit of a chat. Five minutes, that's all.'

The woman sucked her teeth. 'I suppose that would be all right... I am also worried about Mr Whitaker. He is, I think, a very lonely man.' She collected her keys and locked her door.

Rory led the woman into the kitchen of number 11 and began to search the cupboards for tea.

'The name's Rory, by the way. Rory Williams. You're?'

'Mrs Levenson.'

*

His car had been stolen. Or at least, it wasn't where he'd left it.

Mark was a little shaken, but after the rest of the evening's events, he didn't have the energy to get annoyed. He considered finding a phone box to call the police but something made him decide against it. That Doctor and his two friends, they had something to do with this. Something to do with Mrs Levenson not being in Flat 12. He'd find the Doctor, get him to explain.

He returned to the electrical goods shop where he'd met the Doctor, but there was no trace of him. Peering in the shop window, it took a while for him to register what was wrong about the television sets on display. They had all been widescreen and HD, but now they were the old, square type. And the shop sold video recorders! Who the hell sold video recorders these days? Mark looked up at the shop sign. *Dixons*. But there weren't any Dixons any more.

Mark kept walking, his mind a whirl, past the video rental store – wait, hadn't that been a fried chicken restaurant? The posters in the window advertised *Mrs Doubtfire* and *Groundhog Day*. The butchers were still there, and the bookmakers, but instead of the Taste Of The China, there now stood a greasy-spoon café.

Exhausted and hungry, Mark entered the greasy-spoon and leaned on the counter. The menu chalked on the blackboard included a cup of tea for 40p and a bacon sandwich for a quid. Mark gave his order to the café owner, a tired-looking man in his sixties, then sat down at a table where somebody had left a copy of *The Sun*. According to the front page Bobby Charlton had just been given a knighthood.

The date at the top of the page read *10 June 1994*.

'1994?'

The Doctor darted around the six-sided console, adjusting the controls as if trying to achieve a high score on a pinball machine. The floor juddered and swayed and Amy clutched at one of the railings around the console to stop herself from falling to the level below. '1994. Just over seventeen years into the past. Which is *odd*.'

'Odd, in what sense?' asked Amy.

'The Angels usually send their victims forty, fifty, a hundred years into the past,' gabbled the Doctor in a rush of enthusiasm. 'Stick them out of the way somewhere safe, where any minor alterations to the time stream will be absorbed by the established pattern of history.'

'Oh, right,' said Amy, trying hard to sound knowledgeable. 'Time can be rewritten!'

'Time *can*, as you say, be rewritten. Insignificant details can be changed, so long the big picture remains more or less the same. Imagine time as being a great big carpet. Or, on second thoughts, don't.'

'But you said this Angel was different.'

'Yes,' The Doctor peered at the central rotor, tensing his fingers in preparation for a landing. 'It's sent him back to a point *within* his own lifetime. Which I'm afraid is very, very bad news indeed.'

Mark leafed through the newspaper. There were a couple of pages on the forthcoming European elections and speculation as to whether John Prescott or Tony Blair would be the next leader of the Labour Party. As Mark read, a bass-heavy reggae track played on the radio.

Somehow he'd travelled in time. It was impossible, utterly impossible, but there was no other explanation for it. Ever since he'd felt the touch of that statue, he'd been walking around in 1994. It felt strange, almost dreamlike. And yet so *real,* so *mundane.* If it was a dream, he would hardly be able to read advertisements for washing machines, or taste the bitterness of the tea. And besides, if it was a dream, his feet wouldn't still hurt from the run to his flat.

So the next question was, what was he going to do? Would he ever get back to his own time? For all he knew, he was stuck here permanently. He'd have to get a job, find somewhere to live. First things first, he'd have to find somewhere to sleep tonight.

The café owner coughed and indicated the clock. It had gone eleven. 'Closing up, mate.'

Mark rummaged in his pockets for some change and dropped it in the saucer on the counter. 'Cheers. Thanks.' Behind the counter was a black-and-white monitor showing the output of the café's closed-circuit cameras. On the screen Mark could see himself and the café owner, but thankfully no statue.

'What's this?' said the café owner, inspecting the contents of the saucer. 'A *two-pound* coin?'

'What's the problem?'

'*Problem* is, we don't take made-up money here. What is this, Scottish? Haven't you got anything else?'

Mark checked his wallet. He had a credit card and

a debit card. For a moment he considered asking the owner if he could use it to pay, before he realised that chip-and-PIN hadn't been invented. Mark patted down his coat and his hand rested on the bulge of the padded envelope.

It wasn't his money. But if he replaced it as soon as he had the chance, that would hardly be stealing, would it? Mark opened the envelope and removed a fifty-pound note. 'Here, sorry.'

The owner held it up to check the watermark. 'You're lucky we've had a good day. Give us a minute.' He opened the till and dug out £48.60 in five- and ten-pound notes and coins, creating a pile which he handed to Mark.

'You wouldn't know of a bed and breakfast around here, would you?' said Mark.

'Not round here, mate. Your best bet's to head into London Bridge.'

'Yeah, thanks.' Mark headed to the door and paused, turning over the envelope in his hands. It was a bit of a coincidence that he'd received it on the same day as being sent back in time. An envelope containing the one thing he would need to survive in the past. It was too lucky. Too lucky to be a coincidence.

As the café owner disappeared into a back room, Mark returned to his table to study the contents of the envelope properly. Along with 120 fifty-pound notes, all dating from before 1994, there was a handwritten letter. Unfolding it, Mark saw a list of dates from 1994 to 2001 annotated with detailed notes.

It was written in his handwriting. And yet he had no memory of ever having written it.

Mark looked at the first date. *10 June 1994. Arrival.*

He checked the other side of the paper. Halfway down the page, the list became a letter:

Mark.

If I remember correctly, you should be reading this in a café in Bromley in the year 1994. Earlier tonight, you were sent back in time.

How did you get sent back through time? I can't go into that here. But you should know one thing. There is no way back to 2011. You have no choice but to live the rest of your life from this day onwards. It won't be easy, but you have the advantage of knowing the future. Out of all the people in the world, you alone know what tomorrow will bring.

I've included instructions describing what I did when I found myself in the past. Follow them to the letter. And whatever you do, make sure these instructions don't fall into anyone else's hands. Guard them with your life.

Your first step is to use the money to create a new identity for yourself. I'll leave you to decide the details. You'll have to make your own way in the world, just as I did when I found myself in the past.

But make sure you follow these instructions, Mark. Because if you do, remember this:

YOU CAN SAVE HER.

Just as I did.

Yours sincerely,

Mark Whitaker, April 2003.

Chapter 3

11 June 1994

The litter in the high street swirled, caught in a sudden gust of wind, and then, with a grinding sound, a flashing beacon appeared in mid air. A moment later the police-box exterior of the TARDIS materialised beneath it. The Doctor emerged, grimacing in frustration at his wibble-detector. Amy followed him, and sighed. 'We haven't moved.'

'Oh, but we have,' said the Doctor. 'Four-dimensionally. See, *that*.' He pointed to the nearby branch of Our Price. 'In seventeen years' time, that shop – *that shop* – will sell sandwiches and Danish pastries.'

'So this is 1994.' Amy looked around. All the shops were closed but one of them had a clock as part of its sign. 'At approximately five minutes past midnight.'

'The time trace has almost faded. He would've been transported through time, but at the same spatial coordinates. Allowing for the rotation of the Earth, its orbit around the sun, and the solar system's orbit around the Milky Way, of course.'

'Then, er, why isn't he here?'

'He was.' The Doctor approached a small café. Squinting inside, Amy could make out chairs stacked on tables. 'Under an hour ago,' the Doctor continued, shaking his wibble-detector. 'We just missed him.'

'Oh well,' shrugged Amy. 'Don't suppose he's got very far.'

'In *London*?' said the Doctor. 'He could be anywhere within a hundred-mile radius. If he travelled at a hundred miles an hour.'

'Can't you detect him with your amazing egg-boiling gadget thing?'

'No. The trail has gone cold.' The Doctor looked around as though the shops held the answers to the mysteries of the universe. 'We have to find him before he does any damage. The wrong word in the wrong ear and the whole course of human history – pfff!'

'Pfff?'

'Gone.' The Doctor clicked his fingers. 'Not with a bang but with a *pfff*!'

'What makes you think he's going to do any damage?'

'Amy. What would you do if you found yourself trapped in the past? In your *own* past?'

'I don't know,' said Amy. 'I'd... I'd probably look for someone I knew. So I could tell them what's going to happen in the future.'

'Exactly! The wrong word in the wrong ear. The first *pebble* of the *avalanche*! That's the danger with only being sent a short way into the past. If you've been sent back a hundred years, you won't know anyone, you won't know enough about the day-to-day events to make much of a difference, and even if you *do* make a difference, there's plenty of time for history to paper over the cracks. Whereas travelling back seventeen years, you'll know people, you'll know all sorts of details about future events, and any alteration in the *course* of future events is likely to have a direct, dramatic and disastrous impact upon your own personal timeline.'

'Then how do we find him? We don't know where he's going to go, we don't even know who—' Amy stopped as she realised she knew the answer. 'Rory!'

'Yes. *Rory,*' agreed the Doctor. 'He's probably wondering where we've got to.'

The Canary Wharf tower glinted in the morning sunshine. It looked odd, standing alone without its surrounding throng of towers. And out on the Greenwich peninsula, there was no Millennium Dome, just a derelict gas works. Ever since Mark had left his hotel, he had found his attention being drawn to the sights that no longer existed in the future; the tower block that would be demolished to make way for the Shard, the waste ground that would become the site of City Hall.

The most obvious differences from 2011 were the advertisements and those high-street shops which had changed their names or logos. But even the people looked different. Teenagers had their hair tousled like street-urchins or in centre partings. Men wore denim jackets and had their jeans belted higher above their waists. Women had highlights and glossy lipstick. The more Mark looked, the more differences he could see. It was like the first day of arriving in a foreign country, finding everything new, searching for the familiar amongst the unfamiliar.

Apart from the hiss of a teenager's walkman, the railway carriage was silent. It took a while for Mark to guess the reason why; nobody had a mobile phone. There were no laptops, no free newspapers. People just read magazines.

In addition to the eerie feeling of being a man out of his time, Mark's stomach fluttered with nerves at the prospect of the coming encounter. His apprehension grew as the train pulled into Blackheath station and he emerged to climb the hill to his parents' house.

Everything was just as he remembered it. The overgrown bushes that would be cropped back. The lawn that would be concreted over. His mother's Peugeot parked in the driveway.

Steeling himself, Mark strode up the driveway and pressed the doorbell.

A dog barked inside the house. After what seemed an age, a shaped coalesced in the door's frosted glass. The door opened to reveal his mother. Looking younger than he'd seen her for years, her hair still dark brown, wearing her old, plastic-framed glasses.

'Hello, yes?' she said, smiling at him curiously. 'Can I help you?'

His own mother didn't recognise him. She had no idea who he was.

Amy stepped out of the TARDIS and onto the pavement outside Mark's block of flats. Nothing had changed.

Rain splashed in the puddles and thunder rumbled in the distance. She followed the Doctor to the entrance where the remnants of the Weeping Angel had been blown away in the wind. 'Where is he?' muttered the Doctor impatiently. 'I said one hour. Some people are so unreliable!'

'We'll just have to wait,' said Amy, kicking her heels. 'Back inside the TARDIS?'

'No time.' The Doctor retrieved his sonic screwdriver from his pocket and levelled it at the door. The sonic buzzed, glowed green, and every single doorbell in the building rang at once. A dozen bedroom windows lit up as their occupants were roused from their sleep.

'Doctor, Amy, it's you!' crackled Rory's voice through the intercom. 'I'll be right down.' A minute later, he appeared at the door, looking relieved and breathless. 'You took your time!'

'I said we'd be one hour,' said the Doctor, tapping his watch.

'Yeah, I know,' said Rory. 'That was a week ago.'

'Is that all?' The Doctor paused. 'Sorry. Did you say *a week*?'

'I did.'

'A *whole week*?'

'Seven days I've been stuck here, waiting for you to turn up.'

'Oh,' said the Doctor. 'Must have forgotten to correct for temporal displacement. Still, could be worse.'

'Worse?'

'Could've been a month. Or a year!'

'I thought you'd forgotten about me! *Again!*'

'Never.' Amy gave her husband a peck on the cheek.

'So you've been here all this time?'

'Yeah. Seems to be what I do most of the time, wait. Though I did pop back to Leadworth to pick up the post. Just bills, I'm afraid.'

'But if you've been here for seven days, where have you been staying?' asked the Doctor.

'Mark's place. After all, I had his keys.' Rory dangled the keys in his hand. 'And Mrs Levenson next door to keep me company.'

'Mrs Levenson?' Amy narrowed her eyes.

'Old lady, neighbour, she's lovely, but… no,' said Rory hurriedly. 'She just made me cups of tea and chatted about Mark.'

'So what did you find out about him?' said the Doctor.

'Everything I could. He doesn't seem to have been one for keeping scrapbooks or photo albums, but I managed to find a copy of his CV and all the addresses of his friends and family.' Rory presented the Doctor with a folded sheet of paper. 'Not many names. Seems like he kept himself to himself.'

The Doctor read the paper in under a second and handed it back to Rory. 'Right. So, given all this, if Mark found himself in 1994… where do you think he'd *go*?'

'Must be a bit of a surprise, me turning up like this,' said Mark, taking in the living room. The television in the corner, the photos on the coffee table, everything was just as he remembered, except for all the photos of him on the mantelpiece. There were so many. His parents must have put them out when he'd left for university and tidied them away whenever he returned.

Mark sipped his tea but didn't swallow. His throat felt so tight he thought he might choke. He wanted to hug his mother and tell her everything that was going to happen over the next seventeen years, but looking at her sitting in the armchair opposite, her eyes twinkling in a way they hadn't done for years, a contented smile on her lips, he couldn't bear to break her heart.

'And your husband? Patrick, wasn't it? He's out at work?'

'Yes, I'm afraid he won't be back until late, council meeting. It's a pity you'll miss him.'

'Yes, a pity. I'd hoped to, well, say hello and stuff.'

'Particularly with you coming all this way, from, where was it again?'

'Canada.'

'Canada, yes. I didn't know we had relatives in Canada.'

'Very distant. Second cousins of second cousins, that sort of thing.'

'You must be on Patrick's Aunt Margaret's side, we don't know what happened to them.'

'Yes, that's right, Aunt Margaret.' There was an awkward pause. The family dog, a Labrador called Jess, padded in, its tail waggling furiously. It sniffed at Mark's legs before deciding to lick his hands.

'You're honoured,' observed Mark's mother. 'She's not normally so friendly with strangers. You know, you don't sound like you come from Canada. I thought they sounded American.'

'Not from the bit I'm from.' Mark struggled to think of a Canadian city. 'It's a small town, fifty miles out of… Toronto. My father was from England, I picked up the accent from him.'

'He was?'

'He um, died. Ten years ago now.'

'I'm very sorry. And your mother?'

'She's still around. Still, you know, coping. She moved out of the house, to a place by the sea. I think she finds it tough, without dad.' Mark scratched Jess behind the ears. She yawned appreciatively.

'And what about you, are you married?'

'I used to be. My wife, um, died in a road accident back in 2003.'

'In 2003?'

'1993,' Mark corrected himself hastily.

'Oh, your poor thing. It must be so hard for you. Any children?'

'No. No, no children.'

There was another awkward pause. Jess lost interest in Mark and stretched out on the rug. 'So what is it you do for work?' asked Mark's mother at last.

'I'm a solicitor,' replied Mark. Even as the words left his mouth he regretted saying them.

'A solicitor? My son Mark's studying law at university.'

'Is he? Oh.'

Mark's mother stared at him over her glasses. 'You know, you really do look a lot like him.'

'Must be a family resemblance.' Mark took a framed photo of his younger self from the mantelpiece. 'Is this him?'

'Yes, that's him,' said Mark's mother proudly.

'You're right, there is a similarity,' said Mark, studying the photo. 'Reminds me of myself at that age.'

Mark returned the photo to its place of honour. 'So, is he doing well, at university?'

'We think so. We don't hear from him all that often, a phone call every couple of weeks, but you know what they're like at that age, away from home for the first time, it's like they forget that mum and dad exist.'

'I'm sure that's not the case.'

'But he'll be home in a few weeks, and then we'll have him for the whole summer.' Mark's mother frowned. 'You haven't touched your tea. Is it all right?'

'Yes, it's lovely,' said Mark, rubbing the corners of his eyes to hold back the tears. He pretended to take another sip. 'What's he like, your son?'

'Oh, just like his father. Works too hard, every hour God sends.'

The phone rang. Mark's mother heaved herself out of her seat. 'Sorry, if you'll excuse me.' She bustled over to the hallway and picked up the receiver. 'Hello. Yes? Mark!'

Mark flinched, fearing he had been found out. But his mother continued. 'I was just talking about you.' She waved to Mark in the living room. 'A relative from Canada, over here looking up his family tree. Mr... um, sorry, what did you say your name was again?'

'Harry,' said Mark, grabbing at the first name that came to mind. 'Harold... Jones.'

'Harold Jones,' his mother repeated into the phone. 'Looks a bit like you, funny that, isn't it? Anyway, enough of me rabbiting on, was there anything you wanted?' There was a pause and Mark's mother reached for a pen and pad. 'Oh, I see. How much do you need this time?'

Mark watched her from the front room. She looked so happy, so full of optimism. Mark put down his cup of tea and rubbed another tear from his eyes.

'But what does this have to do with Mark Whitaker? Why go after him?' asked Rory.

'The Weeping Angel that zapped him back to 1994 did so for a reason.' The Doctor darted around the console, making adjustments to switches, levers and what appeared to be a bus conductor's ticket dispenser. 'It singled him out specifically. It was working to a *plan*.'

'What plan?' said Amy.

'We won't know the answer to that until we find Mark Whitaker. Then we have to return him to 2011 before he changes history.'

'But why's that so bad?' said Rory. 'You're always saying that time can be rewritten.'

The Doctor gave Rory a hard stare. 'It *can*. But that doesn't mean that it *should*. I can rewrite time, yes, because I know what I'm doing. Whereas a human being, blundering about—'

'Yeah, but you're exaggerating a bit, aren't you? I mean, how much difference can one man make?'

'One man, Rory, can change the whole world. You should know that by now.'

'Oh. OK, we have to stop him.'

'Quite. But we have to *find* him first.'

'So how long are you in the country for?' Mark's mother asked as he stepped out of the front door and onto the gravel driveway.

'Oh. About a week or so.'

'Then it's back to Canada?'

'Yes. You, um, must come and visit.' Mark had given his mother a fake address, hoping she wouldn't be too offended if she spent the next few years sending Christmas cards to a distant relative who never sent any back.

'That would be nice. I'm always on at Patrick to take me on holiday, this might be just the excuse I need.'

'I remember. You never had a honeymoon,' said Mark quietly.

'I'm sorry, what?'

'Nothing.' Mark cleared his throat. 'You should go, you really should, before it's too late.'

Mark's mother frowned. 'What do you mean, "too late"?'

Mark swallowed. The air seemed suddenly thin. 'Nothing.'

'No, you meant something, you wouldn't have said it otherwise. What did you mean?'

'I meant, well, my dad always promised to take my mum on holiday, but one month before his retirement, he had a heart attack. You know, it might be a family thing. You should get dad to go in for a check-up.'

'Dad?'

'I mean, Patrick. Because it's the sort of thing where they can cure it, if they catch it early enough.'

Mark's mother considered this. His words had frightened her. 'You don't know what he's like. Stubborn.'

'My dad was the same. Please. Don't take no for an answer.'

'I'll try my best,' said Mark's mother, giving Mark a wary look.

'Sorry. Anyway. I have to go,' said Mark, putting on a brave smile. 'Lovely to meet you. And thanks for the tea.' He shook her hand. As their fingers touched, Mark's fingers tingled, like he'd received a tiny electrical shock.

'Thank you for coming. Give my love to, er, Canada.'

'Goodbye.' Mark smiled and headed down the driveway. He heard his mother call after him but he didn't dare look back. He couldn't let her see the tears dribbling down his cheeks.

The TARDIS floor lurched and whirled like a bucking bronco. Amy clung to Rory for dear life, while Rory clung to one of the stair railings. The Doctor danced around the console, his eyes gleaming with excitement and madness. 'I think,' he glanced up at the scanner, then tapped out a command on the console typewriter, 'Yes. I think I've found him!'

'Found him? Where?' said Rory.

The Doctor pulled a lever and a map of Great Britain appeared on the scanner. It zoomed in on a point north of London. A glowing green dot slid upwards, surrounded by pulsing circles. 'A source of wibbly time stuff – stop me if I'm getting too technical – is heading north-west.'

'You think that's him?' said Amy.

'A great big paradox just waiting to happen. Who *else* do you think it might be?'

'He's heading north-west?' Rory retrieved the folded

papers from his pocket. 'Wait a sec. According to his CV, in 1994 Mark Whitaker was studying at university in...' He checked the paper. 'Warwick.'

'You don't think he's trying to find his younger self?' said Amy.

'I think that is *exactly* what he is trying to do.' The Doctor examined the scanner. 'Odd thing is, though, he seems to be travelling at about a hundred miles an hour...'

'Tea, coffee, sandwiches?'

'No thanks,' said Mark.

The rail steward gave a polite smile then rattled her trolley further along the carriage. 'Tea, coffee, sandwiches?'

Mark gazed out of the window, watching the fields, streams, roads and bridges rush past in a blur. Small villages and towns slid by in the distance and his reflection floated alongside the train in mid air.

He checked his watch. Another hour or so and he'd be back at university. In his head, he ran over the words he wanted to say. He had so much to tell his younger self.

Mark rubbed his right hand. The tingling sensation seemed to be getting worse. It was probably just a strained muscle but something about it made him feel uneasy. Vulnerable. Like he was being watched.

He glanced outside again. Trees rushed past and power lines roved up and down. And looking up, there was nothing but clear blue sky...

... and a wooden blue box spinning in mid air. It hovered about thirty metres above the ground, whirling and flitting erratically, but always remaining parallel with the train.

It was following him.

Inside the TARDIS, the Doctor, Amy and Rory stared at the scanner, showing the Inter City 125 zooming through the green British countryside. The Doctor adjusted the controls to bring them in closer. 'Might be a spot of turbulence. Time stuff won't let us get too close.'

The Doctor dashed over to the exterior doors and shoved them open. A blustering wind burst into the control room with a roar. Balanced in the doorway, the Doctor whooped with delight like a mariner in a thunderstorm, the breeze whipping at his hair.

While Rory remained at the console, Amy fought her way over to the Doctor, the wind causing her eyes to water. Gripping the doorframe tightly, she leaned out and looked down.

They were flying over the train. Trees and pylons hurtled past just a few feet beneath them. It reminded Amy of the scene in *Harry Potter* where Harry and Ron chased the Hogwarts Express.

'He's on board that train?' shouted Amy over the bluster of the wind.

'No doubt about it,' the Doctor shouted back. 'We're not the only ones who have found him. Look!'

The Doctor pointed down towards the last carriage of the train. Six grey figures crouched on the roof, clinging to it with their bare hands, their wings unfolded. All of them perfectly motionless, like statues.

Chapter 4

The moment of decision had arrived. Our Graham had summarised the three prospective dates' replies, and the girl had made her selection. The audience whooped and applauded as the Two She Could Have Chosen passed by, then the divider slid back, the dates kissed, chose their holiday envelope, and the *Blind Date* theme began.

Watching the show, they'd played the usual game of deciding who they'd select for a date, with Rebecca and Sophie choosing the boys, Mark and Lucy choosing the girls, and Rajeev pointedly refusing to look up from his copy of *New Scientist*. Sophie always chose the boy who most resembled Mark, then paid close attention to Mark's selection to discover what he had liked about the girls.

'This is boring,' declared Rebecca. She uncurled herself from her position on the battered sofa and strode in front of the screen. 'We have to go out or we may actually die of old age.'

'What do you suggest?' called Lucy from the kitchen, scooping the remains of the pasta into the bin.

'I don't know. Go to the Saturday night disco at the union or something. We can't stay in watching telly all night. That's what our parents do.'

'Well, I'm up for it,' said Lucy.

'You're always up for it. What about you, Mark?'

'Don't know,' said Mark. 'Should be getting back to work, really.'

'*Mark* has an exam on Monday,' said Sophie, threading her arm possessively through his.

'Which is a whole two days away,' said Rebecca. 'Look, it's a well-known scientific fact that if you don't take breaks from studying your brain will explode. Isn't that right, Rajeev?'

Rajeev nodded sagely, not looking up from his magazine. 'Fact-o-matic.'

'And if you're gonna be sitting in here watching telly, you might as well go out. Right?'

'*You* can go,' suggested Sophie. 'Me and Mark can just have a night in.' She cuddled up.

'I don't know,' said Mark. 'I kind of fancy getting out of the house.' He smirked conspiratorially at Rebecca, and Sophie felt a surge of jealousy. Rebecca – or Bex, as she preferred to be called – could always twist Mark around her little finger. And he always laughed at Rebecca's jokes, he never laughed at any of the jokes *she* made. Why couldn't Rebecca get herself a new boyfriend, or get back together with Dennis Nice-But-Dim?

'Yes, but we can't really afford it,' Sophie reminded her boyfriend.

'Which is why I suggested the union,' said Rebecca. 'It may be totally lame but it's cheaper than any of the clubs in Leamington.' On the screen behind her Michael Barrymore strutted about advertising chocolate fingers.

'OK.' Mark dragged himself to his feet. 'Union it is. Head off in about half an hour? Bagsy the shower. Oh, and Bex, try not to use any hot water while I'm in there. Being suddenly frozen to death wasn't funny the first time, or the next five times.'

'I don't know,' smirked Rebecca. 'For me, it gets funnier.'

'Promise you won't do it.'

'OK, I promise. If it happens again, it will be a *genuine* accident.'

'But I can't go,' protested Sophie. 'Not dressed like this.' She'd be a laughing stock, going to a disco wearing a chunky jumper and jeans.

'You can always borrow something of Rebecca's, I'm sure she wouldn't mind.' Grinning to himself, Mark clomped upstairs. Whoever had designed their house had had a thing about staircases and had tried to incorporate them instead of hallways wherever possible.

'He was just joking, you know,' said Rebecca tactfully, as if it wasn't obvious that Sophie wouldn't be able to squeeze into any of Rebecca's clothes. Was Mark hinting that he'd find her more attractive if she lost weight? That she should be slim like Rebecca?

'You're welcome to any of my stuff,' said Lucy. 'Probably not your style though.' No, thought Sophie, regarding her friend's army surplus trousers and

Shakespears Sister T-shirt.

'It's all right, I'll cope,' said Sophie. 'Half an hour then.'

'Flatmate outing. Party time, excellent,' said Rebecca. 'You coming, Rajeev?'

'No, I'm good,' said Rajeev. 'Not really my scene. Besides, I promised I'd phone my parents later, so that's my entire evening gone.'

'Suit yourself. Now, if you'll excuse me,' said Rebecca. 'I have to make myself gorgeous. This is going to be a night to remember.'

Their old house, just as he remembered it. Mark had taken the bus from Coventry station to Leamington Spa, the same journey he'd made a dozen times before, and now here he was, standing outside the terraced house he'd shared with Rebecca, Lucy and Rajeev in his second year at university. Seeing it made Mark feel... what did he feel? Excited, yes. Nostalgic, like discovering an old school photo. But with a tinge of sadness, at how much he had lost.

The front door opened and Mark ducked out of sight. Three girls and a boy emerged. Mark's heart stopped. The first girl, an indomitable-looking, dark-haired Goth, was Lucy. Then there was Sophie, his ex-girlfriend, all curves, freckles and a severely cut bob of auburn hair.

And then there was Rebecca. Oh God. She looked perfect. She had long blonde hair and wore a black-and-white top with an Inca design and leggings. Her laughter echoed in the dusky air.

The boy was Mark's own younger self. Short brown

hair, gelled into a parting, John Lennon-style glasses, sallow, red cheeks. Wearing his best Fred Perry shirt. He looked so young, so… innocent. Laughing with Rebecca without a care in the world.

Mark watched them go. He'd have to wait until his younger self was alone; he couldn't talk to him while the others were around. Keeping well back, but feeling highly conspicuous, Mark followed his 20-year-old self down the road.

'So what's the plan?' asked Amy as she watched Mark trail his younger self to the bus stop. The old Mark then held back, keeping his face turned away from the group of students.

'We get to him before he gets to himself,' said the Doctor, ducking back behind the garden wall. 'Before his older self gets to his younger self.'

'You make it sound so uncomplicated.'

'And most importantly, before *they* get to either of them'. The Doctor pointed to the roof of the terraced house from which the young Mark had emerged. It took a while for Amy to realise what he was pointing at. Six stone Angels, perched high on the brickwork like gargoyles.

'But why are they after him, run that past me again?' asked Rory.

'Moths to a flame,' muttered the Doctor. 'If Mark succeeds in changing his own past, he'll create a paradox. Once you've altered your own timeline, the young you won't grow old to become the old you who did the altering. Which creates all kinds of peculiar and nasty side effects, including the release of a vast amount of potential time energy.'

'Which is what the Angels are after!' said Amy, keeping her gaze fixed on the Angels on the rooftop.

'Exactly. Look at them. They're hungry, desperate. Then somebody sounds a *dinner gong*.'

'Um, Doctor,' said Rory, indicating the bus stop. Amy turned to look – to see young Mark and his three female friends clambering on the bus, followed by old Mark. Then, suddenly remembering, Amy whirled back to stare at the building. But the six Angels had vanished.

'Come on!' yelled the Doctor, hurdling the wall and pelting towards the bus stop. Amy and Rory sprinted after him, but they were too late. The bus pulled away and rumbled into the distance.

The Doctor spun on his heel, looking for inspiration. A car approached and the Doctor dived out in front of it. Amy gave a quiet scream. The car screeched to a halt moments from the Doctor, who walked to the driver's window, brandishing the wallet containing the psychic paper.

'Hello. I'm a policeman', he said, gesturing to Amy and Rory to get in the back seat. He then slid into the passenger seat beside the driver, a startled-looking vicar. 'Now, follow that bus!'

The setting sun bathed the students' union building in an auburn glow and stretched the shadows of the students milling about outside. Sophie clung to Mark's arm possessively, holding him back as Bex and Lucy led the way up the walkway to the entrance.

The security guards on the door checked their NUS

cards and then they made their way into the near-darkness within.

The place was heaving. Ahead of them, hundreds of students packed the Market Place, their flushed, sweat-soaked faces illuminated by flashes of green and red from the whirling lamps. The chorus of 'Things Can Only Get Better' thumped out of the loudspeakers and the heady smell of perspiration and smoke filled the air.

They approached the fringes of the dance floor, the territory of those too cool or shy to dance. 'Drink?' said Mark to the girls.

'I'm OK,' said Bex. 'Fancy a bit of a dance first.' Without waiting for an answer, she strode onto the dance floor and started to sway in time to the music, stretching her arms above her head. Mark could only stare in admiration. He could never do that, just walk, sober, onto the dance floor, not caring what anybody else thought. It usually took him half an hour to pluck up the courage. But when Bex danced she looked self-assured and graceful. When he danced, Rebecca told him, it looked like he was wading through mud while swatting at invisible bees.

'I wouldn't mind a drink,' said Sophie, arching a disapproving eyebrow. Oh God, thought Mark. She thought he was staring at Bex because he fancied her. Sophie could be so paranoid sometimes.

'Great, let's go,' said Mark, and together he, Sophie and Lucy squeezed their way through the throng towards the lights of the Mandela Bar.

Mark waited until his younger self had entered the

building before joining the queue. He felt absurdly conspicuous. Here he was, 37 years old, surrounded by students nearly twenty years his junior. They shot him pitying glances and sniggered at his clothes.

Approaching the building, though, brought back a flood of memories. It resembled a car park that had been tipped on its side, a slanted slab of concrete surrounded by shallow terraces. It was austere and angular, but to Mark, it represented one of the happiest times of his life.

But how would he get in? The security guards had already given him some doubtful glances. He'd have to bluff it somehow; pretend to be a worried parent or something.

The crash of breaking glass interrupted Mark's thoughts. Immediately all the students in the queue rushed to the edge of the walkway. The two security guards also peered over the edge. 'What the heck!'

Mark took his chance. As the two guards trotted down the stairwell to investigate the disturbance, he walked calmly to the entrance and slipped inside.

Students! Normally they just stole traffic cones. But now, somehow, this time, they'd manage to steal a whole statue.

Trev looked in every direction for the culprits but there was nobody in sight. Which made no sense. Whoever they were, they'd managed to prop the statue against one of the windows of the union building, with one of its arms outstretched, as though it was in the act of punching through the glass. 'What do you think, Nick?' asked Trev.

'God knows.' Nick crouched beside the statue. 'I think some grave is missing its headstone.'

'But how did they get it here?' They couldn't have dumped it without being noticed. Maybe it had fallen off the roof? Trev scanned the top of the building for any signs of movement.

'Stupid idiots—' Nick gave a startled croak. Trev turned to see what had alarmed him.

The statue had disappeared. Where it had once stood there was now nothing but a clear patch on the ground surrounded by shattered glass.

'I just turned away for a second,' said Nick incredulously. 'Where did the damn thing go?'

Amy, the Doctor and Rory jogged past the Arts Centre and across the road. Ahead of them lay the students union building, its lower windows flashing with multicoloured lights. As they approached, the Doctor slowed, allowing Amy and Rory to catch their breath. 'We're getting close,' he said.

'Close to what?' said Amy.

'A build-up of potential time energy. Can't you feel it?' The Doctor waggled his fingers and sniffed. 'A tension in the air. Like before a thunderstorm.'

'Yeah,' shrugged Rory. 'But I just thought that meant a thunderstorm was coming.'

'A thunderstorm *is* coming,' said the Doctor darkly. 'Unless we stop it. Look.'

A streak of lightning flickered across the surface of the building, scuttling over the concrete like a startled lizard, before fading away to a blue glow.

'What was that?' exclaimed Amy.

'The dinner gong,' said the Doctor. He straightened his bow tie and jacket cuffs. 'Now. I'll need your help. Do I look like the sort of person who goes to university?'

'Sorry. Do you *look* like the sort of person who goes to *university*?'

'Yes.' The Doctor brushed his fringe out of his eyes. He was deadly serious. 'Well? Do I?'

'A bit, Doctor. Just a bit,' Amy reassured him jokingly. 'Maybe not in this decade, but yeah.'

'Just say you're from the Maths department, you'll be fine,' suggested Rory.

'Good. Good. Because that is the *cool* department, and I look *cool*. Right?'

'Exactly,' giggled Amy. 'And for *no other* reason.' She then put her hand over her mouth and made a cough that sounded like 'geek!' Rory laughed but the Doctor seemed not to notice.

They headed down a slope to an underpass where a security guard checked the students' IDs. Rubbing his hands expectantly, the Doctor joined the queue. From inside the building came the muffled thud of music.

The Doctor beamed at the guard and flipped open his psychic-paper wallet. 'Hello. I'm from the Maths department. And these are two of my students.' The Doctor leaned forward to whisper. 'I realise they don't look as cool as I do, but they *are* genuine students, believe me.'

'Whatever,' said the security guard, nodding them in. 'Next?'

Inside the building, the noise was all-consuming. The dance floor bobbed and swelled like a sea of arms and faces. The air felt uncomfortably hot but had an almost tangible sense of excitement. These students were having the time of their lives. Dancing, laughing, snogging, all their troubles forgotten.

The Doctor waggled his fingers expectantly. 'We have to find two people. Or rather, the same person *twice*.'

'You're going to suggest we split up, aren't you?' said Rory resignedly.

'I think...' The Doctor paused, lost in thought. 'I think... we should *split up*. Rory, Amy. You find young Mark, he's probably in there somewhere.' He indicated the heaving mass of students bouncing up and down to 'The Size Of A Cow'. 'I'll find the old one.'

'And when we find him?' said Amy.

'We have to get the two Marks as far apart as possible.'

'As far apart as possible, got it.' Amy offered her hand to Rory. 'Rory, are you dancing?'

'Are you asking?'

'I'm asking, lover-boy.'

'Then I'm dancing,' said Rory, taking her hand. Amy pulled him towards the dance floor with a suggestive smirk.

'Oh, and one more thing,' called the Doctor after them. 'Keep an eye out for the Angels!'

Elsewhere on the dance floor, the 20-year-old Mark hopped and whirled amongst the crowd, all self-consciousness now forgotten. He had a couple of pints inside him and they were playing his favourite tunes at a deafening volume, that's all that mattered. It was the indie section of the night, where things tended to get a little raucous. Occasionally he'd be jabbed by an elbow or shoved off his feet, but that was all part of the fun.

Sophie wasn't enjoying herself. She swayed from side to side as though it was an obligation, smiling only when Mark looked towards her. Rebecca bounced around the dance floor, waving and grimacing to friends. Lucy, meanwhile, had joined a group of fearsome-looking girls near the stage. The last Mark had seen of her, she had been making overtures towards a very pretty Goth with a pierced tongue.

The fade out of 'Baby I Don't Care' gave way to the opening snarls of 'Smells Like Teen Spirit'. The song had a desperate, angry quality, and it felt odd hearing it given Kurt Cobain's recent death, but dancing to it felt like a celebration of his life. But Sophie had clearly had enough, and mouthed to Mark that she wanted to go. The rowdiness was starting to get out of hand.

'Any sign of him?' shouted Amy to Rory, whilst waving her arms in time to the music.

Rory shouted something back she couldn't hear. Somebody jostled him, and he stumbled on one foot, not quite falling.

'What?'

Rory shook his head. 'No! You?'

Amy shook her head. 'No! Me neither!'

'Excuse me, excuse me.' Someone squeezed past Amy. Amy spun around, drawing a breath to protest. A familiar-looking young man gave her an apologetic smile before continuing to weave towards the edge of the dance floor, followed by a girl with a bob of auburn hair.

Mark. It was young Mark. Wow, he was quite good-looking in his day, if a little nerdy. The sort of boy who needed Taking In Hand. Fix the hairstyle and the glasses and you might have something.

'And I've found the other one,' said Rory in her ear. 'Look!'

Rory pointed towards the corner of the first-floor balcony where a man stood surveying the crowd. The same man they'd met in 2011. 'And, um, I think we have, er, bats in the belfry.'

Amy craned her neck to look up at the ceiling, which consisted of triangles fitted together in an isometric grid. Hanging from the ceiling, half-camouflaged against the bare concrete, lit by flashes of red and green from the disco lamps, were the six Weeping Angels.

Chapter 5

Mark searched the crowd for signs of his younger self. He thought he'd caught a glimpse of him a couple of times, but had lost him amidst all the faces.

Watching the students, he felt envious. Envious of their youth, their joy, and all the years they had ahead of them. OK, so this disco was tame compared to some of the nightclubs in Coventry, but they were having fun. And that was what Mark envied most of all.

The smoke machine hissed and the hectic drum-and-bass intro of 'No Good' by the Prodigy filled the hall. Down on the dance floor, the indie kids flowed towards the bars while the dance kids surged in from Rolf's bar. Within seconds they were thrusting and gyrating to the beat, furiously miming big fish, little fish, cardboard box. Green lasers swiped back and forth across the crowd interspersed with bursts of strobe lighting.

Blue lightning flickered around the edge of the parapet, snaking over the edges before fading away.

Strange. He'd never seen a lighting effect like that before. And the tingling in his fingers had grown stronger.

'Looking for someone?' Mark turned to see the Doctor standing on the balcony beside him, arms folded in judgement.

'What are you doing here?'

'Looking for you.'

'How did you get here?'

'Same way as you. Well, not quite the same way. I have my own transport.'

'Your own transport?'

'Which is why I'm here,' said the Doctor. 'To take you back... to the future!' He beamed wildly. 'D'you know, I've always wanted to say that!'

'Three quid,' said the student behind the bar. Mark paid her, then collected his three pints of lager, balancing the plastic containers carefully. The slightest wrong move could cause him to squeeze one of the containers, resulting in a disastrous spillage. It took all of Mark's concentration to wind his way out of the bar area, which meant he only noticed that Sophie was talking when she stopped.

'What was that?' Mark asked her as they reached the quiet area by the change machine and he placed the drinks on a nearby ledge.

'I said I want to go home.'

'You're not having fun?'

'I am. It's just that I've had enough. And you've got revision tomorrow, don't forget.' Sophie squealed in alarm as two students pushed between her and Mark.

'Hey, watch who you're shoving!'

'Mark Whitaker?' said one of the students, a tall girl with long, red hair and beautiful eyes. She spoke with a perky Scottish accent.

'Yeah, yes?' said Mark, turning towards the other student, a friendly-looking bloke in a body warmer with unkempt hair and an apologetic grin. 'Sorry, do I know you?'

'No. At least, not yet,' said the girl. 'But that's not important right now. What is important is that you come with us.' Behind the girl, Mark could see Sophie glowering with indignation.

'What – what for?' asked Mark.

'Friend of yours wants a word,' said the friendly-looking bloke confidentially. 'In private.'

Sophie's mouth opened and closed like a gobsmacked goldfish. 'What friend?' asked Mark.

'You'll find out,' whispered the girl enigmatically. 'It's a surprise.'

'This isn't something to do with Gareth, is it?' Gareth was in the same tutor group as Mark, and had a reputation for playing elaborate practical jokes.

'If I say yes, would that make you come with us?'

'No.'

'Well, in that case, no, it has nothing to do with Gareth,' said the girl.

'That's just what he'd tell you to say. OK, I'll come with you,' said Mark, against his better judgement. In his experience, Gareth's practical jokes were best got over with as rapidly as possible. 'But if this is a rag week stunt, I'm not interested.' He took Sophie to one side. 'Can you hold on here? I'll be back in five minutes.'

'I'm not waiting for you,' pouted Sophie, giving the red-haired girl an I-don't-know-who-you-are-but-kindly-drop-dead look. 'Either you come home with me right now… or you don't.'

Mark couldn't think of anything to say. Sophie shot him a furious glance and walked away.

'I'll find you!' Mark called after her, before turning to the red-haired girl. 'OK, let's get this over with. Lead on!'

The green lasers whirled through the smoke and over the dancers, lending their faces an alien hue. The lightning bolts had become more frequent, crackling over the nearby slot machines.

The Doctor leaned on the parapet beside Mark. 'Let me guess. You're here because you want a quiet chat with your former self?'

'How do you know that?'

'It's what anyone would do in your situation. You want to tell him things to look out for, things to avoid. I don't recommend it, I've seen it tried before, it never ends well.'

'Who are you to tell me what I can or can't do?'

'I told you.' The Doctor regarded him with cool, detached eyes. 'I'm the Doctor. I'm the man who's going to save your life.'

'Save my life? From what?'

The Doctor indicated the balcony opposite. As he did so, the Prodigy track launched into its hyperactive chorus and the lights switched to the strobe effect. The flashing gave everything a jerky, film-like appearance.

On the balcony stood four of the statues, all staring

directly towards him. But, by the flickering of the strobe light, they ceased to be statues any longer. They began to move along the balcony. Two of the Angels stretched over the parapet, searching hungrily for their prey, their necks twisting back and forth, while the other two continued to gaze blankly at Mark.

Something grabbed Mark's arm. He whirled around, to see it was the Doctor. 'Don't worry. They're not going to attack you. At least, not *yet*.'

Amy led Mark and Rory up another winding stairwell, refusing to admit, even to herself, that she was lost. This place was like a maze designed by a madman. Whenever she thought she was getting somewhere, she ended up back where she started. Or somewhere completely different that just *looked* like back where she started.

'Where are we going?' said Mark.

'I told you,' said Amy as they passed the offices for the *Warwick Boar* student newspaper for the third time. 'It's a surprise.'

'You don't know where you're going.'

Amy halted, at the end of her tether. 'OK. What's the nearest way out?'

'Don't ask me, I've never been around here before.'

'What about down there?' suggested Rory, indicating a corridor that branched off to the right. Leaving Mark with Rory, Amy hurried around the corner to see where it would lead.

Two Weeping Angels blocked the way ahead, both frozen in position as they lunged out of the darkness towards her, their mouths open in a vision of hatred.

Amy let out a startled scream and backed away from the Angels, remembering to keep at least one eye wide open at all times. She edged back around the corner and into Rory with a bump. 'No, definitely *not* that way.'

'Up the stairs?' Rory suggested.

Amy glanced towards Rory, to see that he had opened the door to another gloomy stairwell. She nodded as confidently as she could. 'Up the stairs it is.'

While Mark and Rory bounded up the stairs, Amy looked back down the corridor. The two Weeping Angels had turned the corner and stood with their bodies arched, reaching towards her with clawed fingers.

Keeping her eyes fixed on the two statues, and winking her eyes alternately, Amy backed into the stairwell and retreated up the stairs, as carefully and as quickly as she could.

'But I have to speak to him,' protested Mark.

'Of course you do. Never mind the consequences, you just make your *own* life better.'

'It's not like that.'

'Don't you get it? Do you think they sent you here out of the goodness of their hearts? No. They're here now because they think you're going to create a big, juicy, space-time event.'

'I don't care,' said Mark. He'd had enough of the Doctor, and all the heat and the smoke and the noise, and the ever-present prickling sensation in his hand, and those moving statues. He just wanted to be alone.

The Doctor blocked his path. 'Oh, for goodness' sake. If reasoned argument doesn't succeed, you'll leave me no choice but to resort to brute force.'

'What?' said Mark, and the Doctor thumped him in the face.

Mark followed the red-haired girl and the friendly-looking bloke through a fire door and out onto the rooftop terrace. After the heat and stuffiness of the union, it felt good to be outside in the cool night air.

'Rory, keep an eye on the door,' said the girl. 'And whatever you do—'

'Don't blink, I know, I know.' The bloke stared at the fire door behind them, frowning in determination as though expecting to see something burst through it at any moment.

Mark looked around at the empty terrace. 'You've brought me all the way up here just for this? I'm going back—'

'No. You have to stay put,' said the bloke, edging firmly between Mark and the fire door.

'Actually, Rory, I think we might be OK,' said the girl. She peered over the terrace parapet, down towards where two students were emerging from the building. No, they were too old to be students. Someone dressed as an old-fashioned professor was helping a dazed-looking man of about 40 stumble out of the entrance. From this angle Mark couldn't make out their faces, but he could hear one of them singing 'Bohemian Rhapsody' with drunken enthusiasm.

The girl darted over to the stairs that lead down from the terrace, checking the way was clear. 'You wait here. Don't go anywhere. And whatever you do, don't follow us.'

'Follow you? As if! You're mad.'

'Yeah, that's it, we're bonkers. Anyway, got to love you and leave you.' The girl grinned and hurried down the stairs. The bloke gave him a long-suffering smile and disappeared after her.

Mark woke to find himself being frogmarched through the campus, one arm around the Doctor's shoulder. His forehead throbbed. 'Oh God, my head. My head!'

'Had a bit too much. Just taking him home!' explained the Doctor as they passed a security guard. The guard nodded. He'd seen it all before.

Mark began to remember the content of their last conversation. 'What did you do to me?'

'I punched you in the face. I'm sorry, I did it as gently as I could.'

Mark withdrew his arm from the Doctor's shoulder and was about to speak when he heard the sound of approaching footsteps. A moment later Amy and Rory emerged from the shadows, gasping for breath.

'Doctor!' shouted Amy thankfully. 'There you are!'

'Amy. Rory. What about—'

'The other Mark?' said Rory, rubbing his sides. 'We left him on the roof terrace.'

'Good, good,' smiled the Doctor. 'Now we just have to get as much distance between them as possible before—'

'Before?' said Amy.

The Doctor looked back the way they'd come. 'Oh dear. Don't look too happy, do they?' The six Weeping

Angels stood about twenty metres behind them, caught in the orange glow of a street lamp. They were all snarling and clawing at the air.

'Not now you've deprived them of their dinner, no,' deadpanned Rory.

Amy gulped, reached out for the Doctor and Rory's hands, and together with Mark, they arranged themselves so they were all facing towards the Weeping Angels.

'Back pedal! Fast as you can!' said the Doctor, taking a long step backwards, pulling Amy along with him. 'And keeping looking at them! Whatever you do, *keep* looking at them!'

Back on the terrace of the students' union building, the 20-year-old Mark gazed across the university campus, considering his next move. He should go and find Sophie. He could already imagine the argument they'd have. Why couldn't she just have fun? Why couldn't she be more like—

'So this is where you've been hiding,' said a familiar voice from behind him.

Mark turned to see Bex appear through the fire door. 'How did you know I was here?'

'Confession time. I followed you. Who were those people?'

'No idea. They just brought me up here and did a bunk.'

Bex joined him at the parapet. She didn't speak for over a minute, and when she did, she began with a laugh, as though what she was about to say shouldn't be taken seriously. 'While I've got you alone,' she said. 'There's this thing I've been meaning to get your opinion on.'

'Yeah?'

'Something I wasn't sure about.'

'Yeah, what is it?'

'This.'

Bex turned towards Mark and kissed him on the lips. Mark could barely contain his surprise. He'd never thought she liked him, not like that. But here she was, kissing him in a way that could only mean one thing. Her lips tasted of cherry lip balm and were warm and soft. And then, like waking from a dream, it was over.

'*That* was the thing you weren't sure about?' stammered Mark. He wasn't completely sure his feet were still on the ground; he would have to look down to check.

'I just wanted to know what it would be like.'

'And so now you know.'

'Yeah.'

'Revolting, right?' said Mark.

'Oh yeah,' said Bex. 'And for you?'

'I'm feeling a bit sick just thinking about it.'

'Probably not a good idea to do it again, then.'

'No.'

And then Mark kissed her. Longer than the first time, Mark holding her against him, gently stroking the back of her neck. Until, too soon, she released him.

'Nope, still revolting,' sniffed Bex.

'For me too. I really need to brush my teeth to get rid of the taste.'

Bex turned away in embarrassment and brushed her hair behind her ear. 'I'm sorry. I know you're with

Sophie, it's just, well, I don't think she knows what she has. God, does that make me a bitch to say that?'

'Probably but I forgive you.'

'Speaking of which, you should probably go and find her,' said Bex, with a sad smile and Mark realised that the moment, whatever it had meant, had passed, and now it was time to return to reality.

'Doctor, they're catching up!' said Amy.

'Yes,' whispered the Doctor. 'Please let me know when they catch up and kill us, I'd hate not to notice!'

They'd walked backwards for what felt like a mile, bumping against walls and roadside barriers along the way. The problem was, whenever one of the Angels slipped out of sight, it would nip around the buildings in an attempt to cut them off. Now although all six Angels were in plain view, they were so spread out it was impossible to look at more than one at a time. And there were only four of them to do the looking.

'It's no good,' said Amy. Each time she looked back at one of them, it had advanced a little closer, its mouth wide, its tongue tasting the air, its face twisted in an expression of utter evil.

She heard the sound of an approaching vehicle behind her. Its brakes squealed as it slowed to a halt, followed by a hydraulic whoosh.

Amy's back pressed against a glass window. Without thinking, she turned. She'd backed into a bus stop. A warmly lit bus waited at the kerb. Amy spun back to face the Angels. They were now only two metres away.

'Doctor. The bus...'

'OK,' said the Doctor. 'With me, three two one, *move!*'

Amy whirled and sprinted as fast as she could towards the bus. She leapt on board, followed by Rory, Mark, and finally, the Doctor. He patted his pockets while Amy dashed over to the window. The six Angels stood frozen alongside the bus, reaching towards it with outstretched hands. But she could see them all at once, just about. So long as she didn't accidentally blink.

'Hello,' Amy heard the Doctor say to the bus driver. 'You probably want money, don't you?'

Come on, Doctor, urged Amy. Come on! Out of the corner of her eye, could see that Rory was also watching the Angels, so she turned to see the Doctor dig a variety of odd-looking objects from his pockets; a banana, a squeaky rubber telephone, *The Venusian Book Of Calm.*

Mark shoved the Doctor out of the way and handed the driver a banknote. 'Here.'

The driver took the note. 'Fifty quid?'

'Keep the change. It's your birthday.'

The driver shrugged, closed the doors, and the bus jerked forward. Amy watched the Angels through the window, still frozen in the same positions at the bus stop, now grasping towards nothing but empty road.

'We made it! We made it!' whooped Rory.

'We were lucky,' muttered the Doctor as he slumped into a seat. 'But the Angels won't give up.' He looked suddenly very tired, his expression grave. 'No. This has only just begun.'

Chapter 6

12 June 1994

'So what exactly are these "Weeping Angels"?' asked Mark.

The Doctor sliced his sausage and skewered it with his fork. But rather than eating it, he waved it in the air for emphasis. 'The most malevolent creatures in the history of the universe,' he said. 'Nothing gives them greater pleasure than to watch a lesser species suffer. And to them we are *all* lesser species.'

'And they feed by sending people back in time?'

'Usually.' The Doctor took a bite of the sausage. 'But these Angels are different. They feed on time *paradoxes*. The more potential *ramifications,* the better. Ramifications, love that word. Rory, could you write it down for me?'

'Still not your secretary,' Rory reminded him.

'Vacancy's still open.' For a few moments, they all sat in silence in the hotel restaurant, the only sound an occasional clatter of cutlery from the kitchen. 'Which is why,' announced the Doctor, finishing his breakfast, 'which is *why* we have to take you home, Mark Whitaker.'

'But if the Angels want a paradox,' said Amy. 'Why go to all the trouble of bringing Mark here? Why not just change history themselves?'

'Because that would make them a *part of* the paradox, they'd end up feeding on their own timelines. They need someone to do their dirty work for them. That way, they remain outside the chain of cause and effect.'

'What if I *can't* go back?' said Mark.

The Doctor wiped his lips with a napkin and leaned forward. 'What do you mean, "can't"?'

The supermarket bustled with Sunday shoppers, mothers with pushchairs and fathers with trolleys. None of them paid any attention to the blue police box parked beside the *Fireman Sam* ride. But Mark couldn't take his eyes off it. It was the same police box he'd seen flying through the air after his train. The Doctor's time machine.

'Let me get this straight,' said the Doctor, leaning proprietorially against the door. 'You received a letter sent from *your future self*?'

Mark nodded. 'I received it the day I travelled back, just before I met you, and the Angel.'

'How do you know the letter came from you?' asked Amy.

'Because my name was at the bottom.'

'Oh.'

'And it was in my handwriting.'

'In your handwriting,' the Doctor repeated, mulling over each word in turn.

'And so was the name on the envelope.'

The Doctor held out a hand. 'Can I see it? The letter, I mean. Not the envelope.'

'I-I don't have it any more,' stammered Mark.

'You *lost* it?'

'I put it in a safety deposit box. In London. Didn't want it falling into the wrong hands.'

'How very public-spirited of you.' The Doctor gave Mark a dark look. 'So what was in this "letter" written in your handwriting?'

'A list of instructions, telling me things I should do, investments I should make, and things I should do to make sure that history remained on track.'

'Such as?'

'Such as... Well, when I was 22 or 23, I went on holiday to Rome. While I was there I lost my wallet. It had all my money in it, credit cards, everything. I retraced my steps but I couldn't find it anywhere. But when I got back to the hotel, it turned out that somebody had already handed it in.'

'But anybody could've done that,' said Rory sceptically. 'What makes you think it was you?'

'Because there was no way they could've known which hotel I was staying in! I didn't really question it at the time, I was just glad to have it back.'

'So this *letter*,' said the Doctor, 'tells you to be in Rome, on a certain street, on a certain day, so you can pick up your former self's wallet and deliver it to his hotel?'

'Yes,' said Mark defiantly. 'That's it, that sort of thing.'

'A Sally Sparrow survival kit,' muttered the Doctor, ruffling his hair. 'And if you're not there to do it, you'll be changing your own past.'

'Exactly. Which is just what you said I shouldn't do, because—'

'— because it would create a paradox.' The Doctor thrust open the doors of the police box and gestured for Mark to step inside. 'I'll take you there now in the TARDIS.' Within, Mark could see an impossibly large, orange-lit Aladdin's cave, a central altar with a glass column and stairwells leading off into vaulted antechambers. It hummed with energy. Mark was tempted to enter, but held back.

'That wasn't the only thing I had to do. There were others,' said Mark.

'What interests me,' said the Doctor, narrowing his eyes. 'Is why you'd even *want* to stay here in the past.'

'Why I'd want to?'

'Yes.'

'Isn't that what anyone would do, given the chance?' Mark looked to Amy and Rory for signs of support.

'No.' The Doctor paused to examine the *Fireman Sam* ride, having only just noticed it, before continuing. 'That isn't what *anyone* would do. Oh, I grant you, everyone would like to go back into the past for a day or two. Check out some bands, see a few shows, pick up a few first editions. The past is like a foreign country. Nice to visit, but you wouldn't want to live there. So why do *you*?'

'I just do,' said Mark, pausing to decide how much

he could tell them. 'Look, in 2011, I don't exactly have a lot to live for, all right? So I think I have a chance of a happier life if I stay here,' said Mark. 'It is my choice, after all.'

The Doctor leaned over the console, staring at the central column, exhaled and slammed his palm against the console in anger. 'Humans,' he muttered, then turned to Amy. 'You're the same species as him, what do you think?'

Amy considered. She glanced out of the TARDIS doors, to where she could see Mark sitting on one of the wooden benches by the fire engine ride. 'I don't believe him.'

'And you?' said the Doctor to Rory.

'I agree with Amy. I don't trust him either.'

'Nevertheless,' said the Doctor. 'He was right. If he isn't here to fulfil all the tasks in that letter he sent himself... that would be another paradox.'

'If there even *is* such a letter,' said Rory.

'Yeah,' agreed Amy. 'He was obviously lying, it was written all over his face.'

'Perhaps... But the story about the wallet in Rome had the ring of truth about it,' said the Doctor. 'And only he knows precisely where and when to be.' The Doctor flicked a couple of switches in irritation. 'We've got no choice. He has to stay.'

The Doctor, Amy and Rory emerged from the police box, the Doctor looking subdued. 'You can stay,' he announced at last. 'Under certain conditions.'

'What conditions?'

'Number one. Only follow the instructions in the letter you sent to yourself. You are not to influence history in any way. Even the slightest deviation could be *disastrous*.'

'OK, I understand.'

The Doctor peered at Mark. 'Number two. You are not to talk to, approach or communicate with your younger self. Keep out of his way at all costs. And the same goes for any friends, relatives, colleagues or lovers. You cannot have *any* contact.'

Mark felt a twinge of guilt. 'Not to make contact. Right.'

'I mean it. Just one word, one telephone call, one postcard, and you'll alter the course of your own timeline. No. Wait.' The Doctor groaned. 'Who was it? Who did you speak to?'

'No one.'

'No. You *must've* spoken to someone. I detected wibbliness.'

'Wibbliness?'

'It's what first attracted the attention of the Weeping Angel. Who was it?'

'I may have… visited my mother.'

'Your *mother*?' exclaimed the Doctor, opening his mouth wide in astonishment.

'Just to say hello.'

'Just to say hello?'

'Yes.'

'Well, I hope that's all you said. Because if you didn't… ' The Doctor stroked his chin. 'What I think is, you've had a very lucky escape, because whatever you said, it can't have made any significant impact. Or you wouldn't be sitting here right now.'

It took a few moments for Mark to realise the implications of the Doctor's words. What he'd said to his mother, trying to convince her to make his father get a check-up, it hadn't changed a thing. His father would still die in three and a half years' time.

'I recommend you stay as far away from your younger self as possible just to be on the safe side,' said the Doctor. 'Get out of the country if necessary. Belgium, I *recommend* Belgium. And I never thought I'd say *that*.'

'Any more conditions?'

'Condition number three.' The Doctor clapped his hands like a university lecturer warming to his theme. 'You are not to tell to anyone you are from the future. Not even as a joke. As far as anyone from this time period is concerned, you were born – how old are you, Mark?'

'Thirty-seven.'

'You were born thirty-seven years ago. You can keep the same birthday if you like. But you have not travelled in time. If anyone asks, you think the whole notion is just science fiction.'

'Right.'

'You'll need a new identity. I'll leave the details to you. Keep your head down. Don't do anything to arouse suspicion. Don't get married, don't have children.'

'I don't see why—'

'Isn't it obvious?' said Amy. 'Because if you end up getting married to some girl, you might be changing history because she *should've* got married to somebody else.'

'All right, I agree, I agree,' said Mark, so loudly that passing shoppers turned to look at the disturbance. 'Don't get involved.'

The Doctor patted his jacket pockets. 'Do you need money?'

'I have money,' said Mark. 'The envelope I sent to myself contained six thousand pounds.'

The Doctor whistled in admiration then frowned. 'Sorry, is that quite a lot?'

'Enough to last me a few months. Is it OK for me to get a job?'

'So long as it's not Prime Minister, yes,' said the Doctor, breaking into a smile. 'Speaking of which, that letter of yours. You have to remember to send it to yourself.'

'I won't forget. I'll keep it safe, and then send it—'

'No. You mustn't send the *original* letter. That wouldn't make sense. You must make a copy, a handwritten copy, *identical* in every detail. And you send yourself the copy.'

'The copy, right.'

The Doctor tapped out a rhythm on the top of Fireman Sam's fire engine. 'Well, I think that's everything. Oh… and one last thing.'

'Yes?'

'Watch out for the Angels. As long as you behave yourself, you should be quite safe. The Angels are only going to be drawn to you if there's the possibility of a paradox. And if you *do* see the Angels, that means you're on the brink of creating a paradox, so whatever you're doing, stop.'

'You're sure they won't come after me?'

'They're not going to waste energy chasing you unless there's a meal at the end of it.'

Mark wasn't convinced but didn't want to press the point. 'If you say so.'

'Good luck.' The Doctor shook Mark's hand and waited by the police box. Rory gave Mark an encouraging slap on the back, and Amy gave him an encouraging kiss on the cheek.

'Be a good boy,' she said, before following Rory into the police box.

The Doctor lingered on the threshold. 'Don't draw attention to yourself. Don't contact your former self. And *don't,* whatever you do, *change history.*' He disappeared inside, shutting the door after him. The lamp on top of the box flashed and, with a wheezing, groaning sound, the police box faded from view.

He'd convinced them. Mark patted his coat pocket, feeling the reassuring weight of the padded envelope. He opened it and checked the list of instructions, reminding himself what he had to do. First, get a fake ID. He had ready cash, so it shouldn't be difficult.

The fingers of his right hand tingled for the first time since the previous night.

'Thanks for coming with me, Mark,' said a familiar voice. Mark turned to see Sophie and his younger self emerge from the supermarket, both laden with plastic bags full of groceries.

Mark ducked behind the *Fireman Sam* ride, keeping out of sight.

'Don't mention it, good to get out of the house,' replied Mark's younger self. 'Besides, I feel bad about abandoning you last night.'

'You're forgiven,' said Sophie. 'But don't do it again.'

'OK, cup of tea, then back to the exciting world of contract law,' said Mark's younger self. His older self watched him walk out into the car park with Sophie.

The tingling in his hand faded until there was no sensation at all. Suddenly there was a brief flapping sound from overhead like the sound of a large bird taking off, but when Mark looked up at the supermarket roof, there was nothing there.

Chapter 7

2 April 1995

Mark poured the last of the white wine into the plastic cup and lay back on the rug. Above him vapour trails crossed the sky. Trees rustled in the breeze and ducks flapped and quacked on the river. In the distance, Warwick Castle rose from the woodland, imposing, and ancient.

Becky – she no longer liked to be called Bex – lay beside him, tickling his neck with a grass stem. 'So where's Sophie today?' she enquired idly, rolling over to lean on her elbows.

'Gone home to her parents,' said Mark. 'No reason.'

'What do you mean, no reason?'

'I mean, we haven't had an argument or anything.'

'Wasn't suggesting you had.'

Mark took a sip of wine. He hadn't had an argument with Sophie because in order to have an argument, you had to be speaking, and at the moment, they weren't speaking. He'd sent Sophie an apologetic email from the computer centre but had yet to receive a reply.

A couple of joggers bounced past listening to portable CD players. 'What about Anthony?' said Mark. Anthony was Becky's latest boyfriend. He had a face that, in Mark's opinion, resembled a pink potato.

Becky thumbed idly through her battered copy of *Captain Corelli's Mandolin*. 'Rugby match. Said he might join us later, but he won't.'

'Right.' Mark stretched back, trying not to think about Anthony, or Sophie, or work, trying to lose himself in the blueness of the sky.

Becky gave up on her book. 'Forgive me, none of my business, but you're not getting on with Sophie, are you?'

'Yeah, you're right.'

'So what've you done wrong this time?'

'No, you're right that it's none of your business.'

Becky pouted. 'I don't know why you put up with her. Sorry to be blunt, but she makes you unhappy, Mark. It's like, on your own, you're quite a nice guy, but whenever you're with her, you just sit there, *glowering*.'

'Do I?' asked Mark, even though he knew Becky had hit the nail on the head. He didn't enjoy spending time with Sophie any more. It had become an obligation to be endured.

'You should find someone else. Someone you actually get on with.'

'I would, but you're taken, alas, alas,' said Mark mockingly.

'You had your chance, as I recall. That night, on the roof of the union…'

'I remember.' Mark finished his wine. 'God, if Sophie knew I was talking to you like this…'

'What?'

'Oh, she has this idea in her head that I would rather be going out with you.'

'Well, *obviously*,' joked Becky. 'I mean, I'm sane, she's a control freak. Is that why she's always so unfriendly?'

'Yo, dudes,' said Lucy, clumping up to them with a smile and a clinking carrier bag. Despite the heat, she wore her usual black T-shirt, jeans and combat boots. Her girlfriend, a shy, bookish girl called Emma, followed in her wake. 'Did you miss us?'

17 February 1996

'Well, this is embarrassing,' groaned Becky.

Mark was lying in an unfamiliar bed in an unfamiliar bedroom. On the opposite wall hung a Monet print and a cork board pinned with Polaroids of parties, pets and holidays. A window looked out onto the cold, drizzly morning. And Becky was sitting on the bed beside him. He could see her back, so smooth and pale, her shoulder blades, her spine. Then she pulled a baggy T-shirt over her head and tugged on a pair of jeans. 'I suppose, civilised thing, do you fancy coffee? Or tea? We're out of milk.'

'Black coffee's fine.' Mark blinked, his eyes stinging as he'd slept with his contact lenses in. 'What's embarrassing?'

'What do you think? Last night.'

Mark remembered. 'Oh.'

Yesterday had been a bad day. He'd got fired from his job in telesales, a job which he loathed but that wasn't the point, he'd never been fired from a job before. After splitting up with Sophie – at long last – he'd moved in with Rajeev. While he had yet to get a placement with a solicitor since graduating, all his friends still lived in Coventry and the surrounding area. But while they studied for PhDs, he drifted from one dead-end job to the next.

He'd gone to Becky's for tea and sympathy. They'd talked for a while, about Anthony, and how Becky hardly ever saw him since he'd got a job in Manchester. Then Becky had boiled some pasta, he'd popped out to the off-licence, and they'd spent the evening curled up on the sofa watching *Cybill, Friends* and *Frasier*. By the time Channel 4 got to *The Girlie Show,* they'd got to the kissing and unbuttoning stage.

'What are you saying?' said Mark, feeling his stomach churn. 'You regret it?'

'Of course I regret it. Hello! Don't you?'

'No.'

'Thanks,' said Becky sarcastically as she inspected herself in the mirror. 'Thanks a lot, Mark. Make it complicated.'

'Look, I know you're with Anthony, it's just, well, I don't think he knows what he has,' said Mark, echoing something Becky had once said to him. 'Don't worry, it'll stay just between us.'

'There is no *us*. It was just a, just a silly—'

'Mistake?'

'Your word not mine. I was going to say "one-off". Let's just try to forget it ever happened, OK?' Becky whipped the duvet from the bed. 'Now I don't want to be rude or anything, but I think you should go, I've got loads of stuff to do today and don't need you hanging around.'

Mark ran the conversation over and over again in his head, trying to work out where he'd gone wrong, what he should have said. He sat alone in the kitchen, drinking instant coffee, watching *The Chart Show* on Becky's portable television. Apparently The Lighthouse Family felt 'Lifted'. Mark didn't share their optimism and turned it off.

'When you're finished,' said Becky, pausing on her way to the door in a thick coat, scarf and beanie hat, 'make sure the door locks behind you.'

'Don't you think we should talk?' said Mark.

'About what?'

'About what happened.'

'There's nothing to talk about,' said Becky. 'Goodbye, Mark.' She left, the door slamming shut behind her.

Mark finished his breakfast, washed up the mug and bowl, pulled on his jacket, and braved the outside world. Speckles of snow fluttered in the blustery air. The snow wasn't settling, though, it was just melting and making the pavement sludgy and grey.

Something had changed between him and Becky. The warm feeling of trust, of private jokes and shared confidences had been replaced by a feeling as cold as this February morning.

Mark huddled his hands into his pockets and

headed for home, thinking about the fact that he'd lost his best friend in the world.

Inside the TARDIS, the Doctor cranked the dematerialisation handle and darted around the console, making an adjustment here, typing in a new setting there, all the while glancing at a folded sheet of paper.

'So that's it?' said Amy, trying to attract his attention through the glass of the central column. 'You're just trusting him, leaving him in the past?'

'Not quite,' said the Doctor, grimacing as he pulled a particularly stiff lever. 'I'm slaving the navigation systems to the contents of Mark Whitaker's CV.'

'What does that mean?' asked Rory.

'*Curriculum Vitae*. It's Latin. Would've thought you'd have known that.'

'No, what does "slaving the navigation systems" mean?'

'It means the TARDIS is going to follow Mark through the course of his life. Young Mark, I mean. Wherever he is, the TARDIS won't be far away. Multi-dimensionally speaking.'

'You're using the TARDIS to keep tabs on him?' said Amy.

'Which means that if there *are* any disturbances in his timeline, the TARDIS will put us down nearby.'

'Disturbances?' said Amy. 'You mean if old Mark doesn't behave himself—'

'Exactly.' The Doctor nodded. 'If at any point he crosses his younger self's path, or attempts to change the course of history… we'll be there to stop him.'

'But hang on,' said Rory. 'You said that whenever there's a build-up a potential time energy, the Weeping Angels will be drawn to it like moths to a flame.'

'I did,' said the Doctor, suddenly solemn. 'Which is why we have to get to him first.'

16 December 1997

'Mark!'

It took the 24-year-old Mark a couple of seconds to register that someone had called out his name. He turned, searching the shopping precinct for a familiar face. There were pensioners in heavy coats, young families with pushchairs, teenagers with Santa hats and rucksacks, all of them wielding bulging shopping bags. A brass band pumped out a festive carol.

But even with the brisk sense of excitement in the air, even with the silvery webs of lights overhead, even with the combined efforts of Slade, Wizzard and Wham!, Mark didn't feel full of Christmas cheer. He felt numb, miserable and anxious.

Until he saw Becky stride out of the crowd towards him, her face beaming. She wore a fluffy cream-coloured hat and scarf, her cheeks flushed from the cold. 'Mark!' she repeated, before hugging him. 'What are you doing here?'

Mark lifted his two bulging shopping bags. 'Guess.'

'Me too. God, Christmas is a nightmare.' Becky studied his face. 'Something different about you. What is it? Don't tell me. No, I give up, tell me.'

'New glasses,' said Mark, though they weren't new,

he'd got them six months earlier.

'They suit you,' said Becky earnestly. 'Groovy, baby! Look, do you fancy going for a coffee, only I think that if I don't get out of the crowd, I might literally murder someone.'

'Yeah, sounds great,' said Mark. Becky guided him through the crowd, past Woolworths with its cardboard cut-out Teletubbies, and past the large, stone fountain, where the rushing water glittered in ever-changing colours.

Becky paused at the fountain, disconcerted. 'Hey, since when did they put the statues here?'

Mark shrugged. He'd never really noticed them before. Six stone statues of angels in robes, placed around the edge of the pool, facing outwards. Except they were all covering their faces with their hands.

They stepped into the steamy warmth of the coffee shop, to be greeted by the chorus of 'Never Ever' on the radio. 'Coffee?' said Becky. 'Let me remember. Black, no sugar?'

'Yep,' said Mark.

'Grab us a seat, can you, I'll get these.'

While Becky paid for and collected the two cups, Mark found a couple of padded seats in the corner by the window.

'So,' said Becky, carefully placing the coffees on the table, on top of a discarded copy of *The European*. 'News. Tell me everything.' She shrugged off her coat and took the seat opposite. Mark studied her for a moment. She looked different. She'd had her hair cut short and dyed red with a blonde streak, like the girl from *This Life*, and wore more lipstick and eyeliner.

'Not a lot, really,' said Mark. 'Still working for the housing association. Boring but it pays the rent, just about. Still looking for a practice that'll take me on. You?'

'Oh, you know, dissertation rumbles on. OK, that's work out of the way. What about everything else? Are you still with that girl, what was her name?'

'Jenny,' said Mark. 'Yeah, we're still together'. He'd met her on his first day at the Housing Association. They were both temping in the same office and found they both needed someone sane to talk to. Jenny was very... *determined.* It had been her idea for Mark to change his spectacles, along with most of his clothes. Mark sometimes wondered if she even had a sense of humour. Whenever he made a joke she would just look at him as though he had let her down somehow.

'And it's going OK?'

'Yeah, it's good. We haven't moved in together yet but it's, you know, inevitable.'

'Wow. Sounds serious. How long has it been, then?'

'Nearly a year.'

'A year? God, I'm so out of date.' Becky blew the foam off her coffee and took a sip. 'When I last saw you, you'd just started going out. She is the one with no sense of humour, right?'

'Yeah,' laughed Mark. Becky had met Jenny, very briefly, at Lucy's birthday party in March. He could still remember the argument he'd had with Jenny on the way home, it had been their first big argument. The first of many.

But while that had been the last time Becky had seen him, it hadn't been the last time he'd seen her. The last time he'd seen her, she'd been chatting with some people he didn't know at Rajeev's going-home party in July. He'd watched her from the other side of the room but for some reason he couldn't bring himself to go up to her. What would he say? After that night in February, they hadn't had a proper conversation. He always felt self-conscious and resentful and she always gave the impression she would much rather be somewhere else.

'And what about you? Still with Anthony?'

'Oh, yeah. He's still keen, bless him. We're doing Christmas at his parents.' Becky grimaced. 'Which will be *agony*. I don't think they regard me as daughter-in-law material. What about you, what are you doing?'

'I'm going home, to spend it with my parents.'

'Oh, sounds nice.'

'Not really. My…' Then it all came out in a rush. 'My dad had a heart attack two weeks ago, he didn't die, but they've had to take him into hospital for observation, because it might happen again, and so… and so I've taken as much time off work as I can, I'm going down tonight, it looks like he's going to be spending Christmas in hospital, and so I have to be there, not just to see him, but to be there for Mum because, on the phone, she sounds like she's trying not to cry and, so, yeah, that's what I'm doing this Christmas.'

Mark picked up a tissue and rubbed it into the corners of his eyes.

'Oh my God. I'm so sorry.' Becky gave him a sympathetic smile, and suddenly Mark felt like he was with the old Bex again.

'Mum was always on at him to go for a check-up. Apparently some relative in Canada had a heart attack when they were his age. But he never got around to it, always too busy. Anyway, Christmas shopping,' said Mark, swallowing the lump in his throat. 'What a nightmare, eh?'

'Yeah,' said Becky, rubbing his fingers. 'Look, if ever you need someone to talk to…'

Mark felt the touch of metal, and looked down to see the engagement ring on Becky's finger. Becky saw that Mark had noticed it and withdrew her hand.

'"Not daughter-in-law material",' said Mark. 'I should've picked up on that. Congratulations.'

'Thanks.'

'So when's the wedding?'

'Oh, not for ages. Anthony's parents want to organise this massive do. They've actually been watching *Four Weddings* on video and taking notes. I think they're waiting on St Paul's cathedral becoming available. You're invited. Obviously. You and what's her name, Jenny. If you're still together.'

'What is it with you and trying to split me up with my girlfriends?' joked Mark.

'I just think none of them are good enough for you, that's all.'

'Yeah,' said Mark. 'Which reminds me.' He dug in his pocket for his new mobile phone and switched it on. One missed call, one new message. From Jenny, telling him to meet her at her office at four, that she loved him and not to be late, x. Mark checked the time. Half past four.

Mark finished the rest of his coffee. 'Look, I've got to go, it was lovely seeing you, Becky.'

'Lovely seeing you too, Mark. One thing you should know before you go, though.'

'Yeah?' Mark pulled on his coat and grabbed his shopping bags.

'No one calls me Becky any more. It's Rebecca.' She stood up as though to shake his hand. But instead she laughed and gave him a stiff hug. 'And what I said, about phoning me, any time, I meant it. Oh, and you left your paper.' She handed him the discarded copy of *The European*.

'Not mine.'

'Oh,' she said, taking it back. As she did, a lottery ticket slid from its pages. Rebecca examined it. 'Hey, it's for tomorrow.' She pressed it into his hand. 'You have it. You never know.' She put on the deep voice of the television advert. '"It could be you".'

Mark slipped the ticket into his pocket. 'Yeah. Anyway. Have to, you know.' He walked over to the door and out into the chilly, damp and oh-so-Christmassy shopping precinct.

But he couldn't help looking back at Rebecca, sipping at her coffee in the window. And then he noticed a tingling sensation in his right hand, the same feeling he'd had on the night they'd first kissed.

Rebecca drained her coffee, thinking about Mark. He looked like he hadn't slept for days, his eyes were red from crying and, God, those glasses really didn't suit him. She'd wanted to kiss him and tell him everything would be all right, but she'd held back.

And then she noticed the man standing at her table.

For a moment she thought Mark had come back, until she realised it wasn't him. The man looked familiar, but she couldn't place where from. He looked about 40, with a deep tan and tinted glasses. 'Forgot my paper,' he said, collecting *The European* and turning to go.

'Hey,' said Rebecca. 'There was a lottery ticket, I'm sorry, my friend took it, we thought—'

'It's OK. He probably needs it more than I do.' The man smiled and left, just as the coffee shop radio began to play the opening chords of 'Angels'.

Chapter 8

11 August 1998

'Mind if we join you?' asked Amy.

'No, not at all,' said Mark, sliding a chair towards her. 'I thought I might see you here.'

Rory let Amy take the seat with the most shade, while the Doctor eased himself into a chair directly in the glare of the midday sun. The narrow street baked in the heat, heady with traffic fumes and swarming with tourists. Occasionally the guttural rev of a motor scooter drowned out the chatter from the coffee bars and souvenir stalls, but it never drowned out the constant, thunderous, splashing roar of the Trevi Fountain waterfall.

'Three frappuccinos,' the Doctor told the waitress. 'Make mine decaffeinated.' The waitress boggled at the Doctor. His only concession to the heat was a pair of sunglasses. He should have been roasting in his tweed jacket and bow tie, but showed no discomfort.

'How did you find me?' asked Mark.

'Wibbliness,' explained Rory. 'The Doctor has a special detector.' The device lay in the Doctor's lap, bleeping intermittently.

'Oh, yes, I remember,' said Mark. 'When we first met. It seems such a long time ago.' Rory exchanged a raised eyebrow with Amy. As far as they were concerned, they'd only left Mark at the supermarket a few hours ago, yet he already looked noticeably older, his hair thinning, his skin tanned but showing deeper lines around his mouth and eyes.

'How long has it been?' asked Amy.

'Four years. I'm 41 now.' Mark sipped his tea and smiled. 'While you're not a day older.'

'So what have you been up to? Whatever it is, you're looking good on it,' said Rory, referring to Mark's finely tailored grey suit.

'Behaving myself,' said Mark with a curt smile. 'Keeping out of the way of my younger self. I've been travelling – I did spend a few weeks in Belgium – and now I have my own small business consultancy company.' He presented the Doctor with his card.

The Doctor read the card. '"Harold Jones". Your new identity?'

Mark nodded. 'Seemed to fit the bill. Nice and anonymous, nothing to provoke suspicion.'

'And what sort of "business consultancy" do you do?' said the Doctor, pocketing the card.

'Don't worry, I'm not giving them information about the future or anything like that. It's just a cover for my investments.'

'Investments?'

'I've done quite well for myself over the past few years, Doctor. Oh, I've been careful not to draw attention to myself – for each deal that makes a profit, I make sure I make another that makes a loss. So far I've mostly been dealing in internet start-ups, registering domain names and so on, but recently I've moved into property, share options, and, ah, West End musicals.'

'West End *musicals*?' exclaimed Amy.

'I'm putting some money into an ABBA thing that's coming up. I think it might do well.'

'Are you a big fan of musical theatre, then?'

'No, but I know which shows will still be running in ten years' time. It's the same for all my investments; if I know a company is still around in 2011, I buy shares in it. Surprising how easy it is to make money, if you know the future!'

The waitress delivered their chilled coffees. The Doctor waited until she had gone before resuming their conversation. 'So what about your little to-do list? How's that been getting on?'

'See for yourself.' Mark took a sheet of paper from his briefcase and handed it to the Doctor.

The Doctor absorbed both sides in under a second. 'This is the letter from your future self?'

'No, this is the copy. The original is kept in a safe in my flat.'

'Very wise.' The Doctor returned the letter. 'Already ticked two items off the list, I see.'

'Yes. I had to delay the start of one of my third-year exams, because my younger self was running late. And then last year I had to make sure he ended up with a winning lottery ticket.'

'A winning lottery ticket?' said Rory, his jaw dropping.

'Not the jackpot. Just matching enough numbers to win about sixteen thousand pounds.'

Amy whistled in admiration. 'Not bad for a day's work!'

'But how did you do it?' asked Rory. 'All the stuff with musicals and internet sites I get, but you couldn't possibly remember what the winning lottery numbers were, one week in 1997!'

'He wouldn't need to,' said the Doctor between slurps of his frappuccino.

'Why?'

'Because he *wrote them down in the letter he sent himself!*' exclaimed Amy with a grin.

'Eh?' said Rory. The more he tried to figure it out, the more confused he got. No, it was no good. A diagram would be required.

'Which brings us to item number three,' said the Doctor. 'Speaking of which, here they *are*... bang on schedule!' He lowered his sunglasses to peer towards the fountain.

Rory followed his gaze – to see young Mark, in a T-shirt and a floppy white bucket hat, wandering through the crowd with a girl in a summer dress. Even from this distance, Rory could tell she was stunning.

So could Amy, who gave Rory a look which in no uncertain terms reminded him that he was now a married man.

For the first time in what seemed like years, Mark felt at peace. The sky was blue, the air was balmy and breezy, and he was with Rebecca. They'd spent the morning exploring the Castel St Angelo, the Piazza Navona, the Pantheon, winding through endless streets, never hurrying but always excited at what was around the next corner. It had been the most perfect day ever.

Of course, he wasn't *with* Rebecca, not in the boyfriend-girlfriend sense. They were on holiday as friends and nothing more, that had been agreed in advance. Although they shared a bed, they shared it with a pillow between them, and were changing into their night things in the bathroom to avoid embarrassment.

How had he ended up in Rome with Rebecca? If he'd known in January how things would turn out... it wouldn't have made it any easier. His father hadn't lasted into the new year, and he'd ended it with Jenny a few weeks later. He just wanted to be a good son to his mother for once. They talked about Dad, Mark hearing stories he'd never heard before, about how they'd first met, and how his father had rushed out of a council meeting to see his newborn son, and how proud he was of him, how he always told everyone he met how proud he was of his son.

He'd remained in contact with Rebecca, talking almost daily on the phone. And she had been great. She always listened, asking questions and making suggestions, even making him laugh.

In April, it was Mark's turn to be the shoulder to cry on. Rebecca had discovered that her fiancé Anthony had been having a relationship with one of his colleagues from work, and that it had been going on ever since he'd moved to Manchester. When she confronted him about this, Anthony begged forgiveness, but Rebecca couldn't forgive him. She could barely look at him without feeling sick.

But she had already booked a holiday in Rome and now had no one to go with. It hadn't been Mark's idea to offer to take the spare ticket. It had been his mother's. She reminded him how his father had never found the time to take her to Paris, and that he'd always regret it if he let this opportunity slip through his fingers.

Mark plucked up the courage to ask Rebecca if she'd mind if he went with her. She laughed and told him that she'd been waiting for ages for him to get the hint. He insisted on paying for his half of the holiday; after all, after his win on the National Lottery, he could afford it.

He'd come so far in the past six months, out of the darkness and into the light. And as though she knew what he was thinking, Rebecca took his hand, and together they squeezed through the crowd towards the Trevi Fountain.

And Mark's right hand began to tingle.

The couple reached the terrace at the top of the steps leading down to the turquoise pool, then paused as the boy took the girl's photograph. Rory, the Doctor, Amy and Mark watched from their table, peering out from behind their menu cards.

'You think you lost your wallet here?' said the Doctor.

'That's what I remember. According to the letter, it should happen any second now.'

Rory edged forward to get a better look. He could see the wallet bulging in the young man's back pocket.

But he couldn't see how it could accidentally fall out. Until he noticed a thin, seedy-looking teenager sidling through the crowd, the only person there not to be gazing in wonder at the statue of Oceanus. Without breaking his stride, the teenager lifted the wallet from young Mark's pocket and walked casually away. Towards where they were sitting.

The Doctor gave Rory a nod. In a few seconds the thief would be within reach. Rory psyched himself up to grab him. But then the thief noticed that they were looking at him. He launched himself into a run, shoving them both out of his way.

Rory turned to see the teenager skidding down a side street. Without thinking, Rory sprinted after him, giving a yell of 'Stop! Thief!' Around him, the tourists gawped on in bemusement.

Rory turned down the side street to see the teenager knocking aside any bystanders that impeded his progress. Ahead of him a Fiat blocked the entire width of the street. The teenager didn't slow down. He simply leapt onto the car's bonnet, ran across its roof and jumped to the ground, making his escape. Without pausing to think, Rory scrambled over the car after him, trying his best to ignore the blasts from the horn and the barrage of insults from the driver.

The teenager darted down another side street, glancing back to see if he'd lost his pursuer. He hadn't. After landing heavily on the tarmac, Rory redoubled his speed, ignoring the stitch in his side. He chased the teenager through a number of increasingly narrow alleyways, if not by sight then by the sound of the teenager's heels.

The next alleyway ended at a flight of steps. The teenager had already climbed twenty or so of the steps but Rory didn't give up. Groaning with the effort, Rory raced after him. The steps were incredibly steep, rising up over the rooftops, and just when Rory thought they might go on for ever, they ended at a car park.

The teenager dashed over to a motor scooter, but before he could turn the ignition, Rory lunged at him, knocking both the thief and his scooter to the ground. In the struggle that followed, Rory prised the thief's fingers apart and wrenched the wallet out of his grip. Then the teenager shoved Rory aside and, shouting expletives, scurried into the distance.

Rory lay on the tarmac, his chest heaving, until he heard the Doctor jogging up the stairs after him.

'Well done,' said the Doctor, helping him to his feet. 'You've just saved the entire space-time continuum.'

'Great,' said Rory with little enthusiasm, handing him the wallet.

The Doctor examined it and shook his head. 'But I'm afraid it's the wrong wallet.'

'Wh-what?'

'Only joking,' beamed the Doctor. 'It's the right wallet. Your *face*!' The Doctor adjusted his bow tie, feeling terribly pleased with himself. 'Now, we have to deliver it to Mark's hotel…'

It had been one of the best mornings of his life, only to be followed by one of the worst afternoons. Somewhere between the Pantheon and the Trevi Fountain, Mark had lost his wallet. The wallet containing all his money, his credit cards, his travel insurance, everything.

They spent the next hour retracing their route, Mark scanning the gutters whilst cursing his own stupidity. He knew Rebecca didn't have enough cash to pay for both of them. They wouldn't be able to go out, or visit the museums, or see Hadrian's villa at Tivoli. The more Mark thought about it, the more furious he got.

As they reached the Pantheon, Mark slumped against a wall. 'OK. That's it. I give up.'

'Oh well,' said Rebecca. 'Never mind.'

'I don't get you. I'm going out of my mind here, and you're just taking it all in your stride.'

'I'm on holiday. It's not as if Rome is going anywhere. And anyway, what's the point in me worrying when you're stressing out enough for both of us?'

'So you're not angry with me?'

'Of course not. Look. Let me buy you an ice cream.'

'We can't afford it.'

'OK, let's... let's walk back to the hotel, I might still have some traveller's cheques in my suitcase. We can at least work out how much money we have left.'

'Yeah. I suppose that's a plan.'

'It's a brilliant plan, because I thought of it,' said Rebecca, teasing a smile out of him. 'And don't worry. So you lost your wallet. It's not the end of the world.'

The Doctor twirled the wallet in his hand like a magician with a playing card before handing it to the hotel receptionist.

'Look, here's a thing. I found this wallet lying in the street and I think it might belong to somebody staying in this hotel.'

The receptionist opened the wallet, then looked

at the Doctor as though he should be arrested for interrupting her day.

'Mark Whitaker,' said Amy clearly and helpfully. 'His name was on his credit card.'

'Yes,' said the Doctor. 'So if you could put it aside, for when he gets back. That's all. And if he asks about me, just say it was some… handsome stranger.' The Doctor adjusted his bow tie proudly.

Amy tugged the Doctor away from the receptionist before he embarrassed her further, to join Rory and Mark in the street outside.

'Well, that's that finished,' said Rory as Amy placed a congratulatory arm around him.

'Yes. Another one to tick off your list, Mr Whitaker.' The Doctor squatted on the ground, opened his leather satchel and took out his automatic wibble-detector. 'Except…'

'Except what?' said Mark.

The Doctor held the device above his head, like someone trying to get a better phone signal. 'I'm still getting wibbliness. You see that dial?'

Mark peered at the machine. 'The one that isn't actually moving?'

'Yes. The fact that it isn't actually moving means that the course of history is still in flux.'

'But we delivered the guy's wallet,' protested Rory. 'What else do we have to do?'

'There's nothing else in my letter,' said Mark.

'Then it must be something else,' said the Doctor, waggling his fingers. 'Something *else* that happened on this day. Something with lots of… what was the word, Rory?'

'Ramifications?' sighed Rory.

'Ramifications! Yes. Something with lots of *ramifications*! So, Mark, what was it?'

'You can't expect him to remember,' laughed Amy. 'As far as he's concerned it was, like, fifteen years ago!'

Mark ran a hand through his hair, smiling at a reawakened memory. 'Oh no, I remember like it was yesterday.'

'But it's not yesterday. It's *today*.' The Doctor gripped Mark by the shoulders and looked directly into his eyes. 'So tell me, after you recovered your wallet... what did you do next?'

Chapter 9

The disembodied heads of long-dead Roman Emperors lined the hallway, each one made of smooth, white marble.

'And this one is,' said Rebecca, reading the plaque beneath it. 'Tiberius. On a scale of bonkersness from one to ten, he was about an eight.' She continued down the Hall of Emperors, her footsteps clicking on the marble floor.

It was nearly closing time and the Capitoline Museum was deserted. Mark relaxed, breathing in the refreshingly cool air, scarcely able to believe they were here after all the traumas of the day.

When they'd finally made it to the hotel, the receptionist had greeted him with wide-eyed excitement, waving and shouting his name. She had his wallet and it still contained all his credit cards and money! According to the receptionist, it had been handed in by some 'handsome stranger'. Mark thanked her effusively, promising her that when he got home he'd tell everyone he knew that Italians were the most honest people in the world.

What it didn't contain was any details about his hotel. So how could they have known where to hand it in? Mark was too relieved to question his good fortune. He and Rebecca bought a celebratory pizza and resumed their tour, visiting the Colosseum, the ruins of the Roman Forum and the Palatine Hill, before climbing the steps to the Capitoline Hill. As they entered the museum, they persuaded a Korean tourist to take a photo of them beside Constantine's *Monty Python*-esque foot before entering the palatial interior.

'Weird,' said Rebecca, interrupting Mark's thoughts. 'Don't look very Roman, do they?'

Rebecca indicated six statues standing in a line against the wall. They were statues of angels, their arms crossed over their chests, their eyes staring worshipfully upwards. With their robes and nest-of-vipers hair, they resembled the statue of a Wounded Amazon from the Great Hall. But their wings looked anachronistically Victorian.

'What do the labels say?' said Mark, giving each statue no more than a cursory glance.

'There aren't any,' said Rebecca. 'Guess they must be new.'

Young Mark and Rebecca inspected the statues for a few more moments before disappearing through the doorway at the far end of the hall.

'Weeping Angels,' sighed Rory.

Gesturing to Rory, Amy and Mark to stay crouched behind a bust of the Emperor Hadrian, the Doctor approached the statues, holding his eyes open with his fingers, his steps not making a sound. 'Yes. That proves it.'

'Proves what?' whispered Amy.

'They're waiting for a paradox to happen.' Blue lightning crackled across the ornate ceiling.

'What sort of paradox?' shivered Rory. 'I mean, caused by what?'

The Doctor turned to Mark. 'When you were here before, did anything happen that was unusual in any way? A stroke of fortune, a coincidence that set you down a particular path?'

Mark thought back. He remembered visiting the museum before, and seeing the Angel statues had jogged a memory of having seen them before, but after that, he couldn't recall anything apart from the conversation he'd had with Rebecca on the balcony overlooking the Forum.

'Nothing springs to mind,' said Mark, then he slapped his cheek. 'Oh! Except there was one thing. We got locked in.'

'You got *locked in*?' said the Doctor.

'Er… Doctor,' said Amy quietly. 'You're not looking at the Angels.'

'I thought you were,' said the Doctor. 'Do I have to tell you to do everything?'

'I am. *Now*.' said Amy, staring, wide-eyed, in the direction of the statues. Mark followed her gaze. Three of the statues were caught in walking poses, heading for the doorway after young Mark and Rebecca. The other three had been frozen as they stalked towards the Doctor, their arms outstretched like sleepwalkers, their features calm and blank.

'They're trying to get between us and the young Mark.' The Doctor walked towards the Angels, beckoning to Amy, Rory and Mark with a finger behind his back.

'You keep an eye on the ones near us, I'll keep an eye on the others,' whispered Mark. With Amy and Rory treading silently behind him, he crept after the Doctor, keeping his eyes fixed on the Angels heading for the doorway, resisting the urge to turn towards the ones only a few metres away. Slowly but surely they made it past the statues to the doorway. The moment they were all through, the Doctor slammed the door shut behind them and secured it with his sonic screwdriver.

'So, Doctor,' said Rory with a sigh of relief. 'What exactly is it we have to do?'

'Isn't it obvious?' said the Doctor with a wild-eyed grin. 'We have to lock young Mark in!'

'Five minutes, no more, OK?' said the museum guard, barely sparing Mark and Rebecca a glance before he disappeared into the toilet with an urgent shuffle. They were in the underground tunnel that linked the two halves of the museum, and which led to the Tabularium, the ancient Roman record office. They wandered through a hall filled with altars and burial slabs into a rough-walled tunnel which opened onto a cloister overlooking the remains of the Forum below, the toppled Corinthian columns, and, in the distance, the Colosseum. All bathed in the coppery glow of the setting sun.

Rebecca rushed over to the balcony, sighing in awe.

'What a view!' She turned to Mark and smiled. 'I'm glad you came along in the end. This wouldn't have been half as much fun without you.'

'You call watching me panic for an hour *fun*?'

'Well, entertaining,' she smirked.

Mark snapped a photograph of the view. 'Come on, we should be heading off.'

'Let them chuck us out. I want to see what's down here first.' Several passages littered with temple fragments branched off from the cloister. Rebecca ran off to explore the first while Mark glanced back down the tunnel to the Tabularium. For a moment he thought he'd seen a movement in the corner of his eye, as though they were being followed, but there was nobody there.

'That was close,' whispered the Doctor. They all stood flat against the tunnel wall, as still as statues, the Doctor and Mark on one side, Rory and Amy on the other. Rory could feel the clammy bumpiness of the stone wall against his back.

When the young Mark had slipped out of sight, the Doctor relaxed and stepped forward. 'If your younger self sees us...' He pulled a face to indicate an unspecified calamity.

They proceeded towards the narrow doorway that led to the cloister. 'Is this it?' asked Rory.

Mark nodded. 'Yes, I remember, we were locked out on the balcony, just through here...'

'Right, well, suppose we'd better get on with it then,' said Rory, reaching for the heavy, iron door. 'I would ask how we're supposed to lock it without the key, but—'

'Sonic,' said the Doctor, rotating his screwdriver in the air.

'Yeah, always the sonic.' Rory began to heave the door when an angry shout came from down the tunnel.

'Hey, what you doing?' The security guard waddled towards them, a tanned man in his fifties with a bushy moustache and the uniform of a much slimmer man. 'That's my job.'

'Sorry, sorry,' said the Doctor genially. 'Just worried about *security*. Can't be too careful.' He swept his sonic screwdriver through the air as though trying to locate invisible thieves.

The security guard squinted at Mark. 'I thought there was two of you?'

'There were,' said Amy perkily. 'But now there are four of us. What of it?'

The guard snorted and heaved the door shut with a bang. He locked it with a set of heavy iron keys before turning to direct them down the tunnel with his thumb. 'Closing time now. Way out is on right, you go up stairs, you go home, I go home, bye bye.'

'Yes, excellent plan,' said the Doctor, clapping his hands. 'Well done. Thank you very much, you have been *magnificent*. Come on, Mark, Rory, Amy. Nothing more for us to do here…'

'Well?'

Mark shook his head. 'No. We're locked in.' The fingers in his right hand tingled, presumably the result of him slamming his fist against on the door.

Rebecca regarded him with amusement. 'Not really

your day, is it?'

Mark didn't know whether to laugh or cry. On the flight out, he'd had this insane fantasy that something might happen between them on this holiday. That she might see him as something more than just a friend. But today she had only seen him at his worst, at his most irritable and incompetent. His one chance to impress her and he'd blown it.

'I'm sure someone will find us,' Rebecca reassured him. 'There are worse places to be locked in. And worse people to be locked in with.'

'That was it? That was all we had to do?' said Amy, strutting after the Doctor.

'I think so, yes.' The Doctor checked his wibble-detector as they climbed the stairs into a gloomy hall lined with statues of mythical figures. 'I'm losing wibbliness. The future's no longer in the balance.'

Mark noticed the tingle in his hand had started to fade. He'd almost forgotten it was there.

'Um, Doctor,' said Rory warily. 'If that's the case, aren't the Weeping Angels gonna be a bit cheesed off?'

'Very,' said the Doctor, as they passed down the hall, their footsteps echoing in the darkness. As the hall had no windows or skylight, the only illumination came from the electric lights. 'So keep an eye out for them.'

Amy looked around, apprehensively studying each statue in turn. Of all the places for a statue to hide, it would have to be a museum filled with statues. 'But we're safe, so long as we see them before they see us?'

'You're never *safe* where the Weeping Angels are

concerned,' muttered the Doctor darkly.

'Behind us,' cried Rory, pointing. The six Weeping Angels stood at the top of the stairs at the end of the hall. All frozen in the process of lowering their hands from their faces.

'Everyone look towards the Angels,' said the Doctor. 'We'll be absolutely fine so long as...'

K-chunk! K-chunk!

The electric lights at the end of the hall flickered and went out. Rory yelped in surprise.

'You had to say it, didn't you?' muttered Amy sharply to the Doctor. 'You had to say it!'

K-chunk!

'Keep moving,' said the Doctor. 'Just keep moving!'

Amy and the others slowly backed away as the lights in the middle of the hall went out. Now the only remaining lights were those behind them. In front of them, Amy could make out the sinister, shadowy shapes of the statues of centaurs and nymphs, knowing that somewhere in the blackness the Angels were lurking, waiting for the final set of lights to go out.

K-chunk!

The final set of lights went out. It was as if Amy had closed her eyes. Somebody grabbed her by the wrist and she gave a tiny scream, until she realised the hand belonged to Rory. A moment later she heard a high-pitched buzzing sound and the Doctor's sonic lit up with a green glow.

The Doctor swung the sonic ahead of him like a torch, revealing an Angel as it lunged out of the darkness towards them. The Doctor flashed the light to the left, to halt another Angel as it reached out with scratching fingers. And another, its mouth wide in a silent scream. He flitted the green light between the Angels, trying to hold them back, but each time he lit one up, it had taken another step towards them.

'Amy, Rory, Mark! Move! Move!' yelled the Doctor. 'I'll hold them off for as long as I can.'

'What about you?' cried Amy

'I'd be extremely grateful if, on your way out, you could get someone to turn the lights back on.'

Amy felt Rory squeeze her hand and, together with Mark, they backed down the hall, watching the feeble green light as it darted back and forth between the enraged faces of the Angels. Then they reached the next room and broke into a run.

'Sorry about all this.'

'What are you apologising for?' said Rebecca, still enchanted by the view. As the sun had set, the colour of the ruins had shifted from orange to a dusky red. The air smelt of ancient ruins and pine trees. 'Besides, how many people get to see this? Luckiest thing, being locked in.'

'It's been a lucky day, overall,' said Mark, joining Rebecca at the balcony. From here, there wasn't a single modern structure in sight. No office blocks, no street lights, nothing.

'Yeah,' laughed Rebecca. 'Must be fate.'

'Can I ask you a question?'

'Go for it.'

'All the stuff that's happened today, anyone else would've been mad at me, but you... you were OK about it. Why?'

Rebecca swept back her hair while she considered her answer. 'Seriously? The way I see it, after what happened with Anthony, I could've got all paranoid and bitter. But then he'd have won, he'd have changed me into a worse person. And after hearing you talk about all the stuff you've been through, with your dad and everything, it kind of put my woes into perspective. Life's too short to be miserable, basically. If you can be happy, then *be* happy.'

'Seize the day?' said Mark.

'Exactly. Seize it, baby.' Rebecca turned towards him with an expression he'd seen once before, on the terrace of the students' union.

His stomach trembling, Mark leaned forward and kissed her.

Rebecca responded, kissing his lips as he kissed hers, gently, precisely, before finally pulling away. 'That's not quite what I meant,' she said.

'No?'

'No. But it's a good start.' Rebecca gave him a conspiratorial smile. 'You know, we could very easily be locked in here all night...'

Back in the hall of statues, the Doctor was fighting a losing battle. No matter how rapidly he alternated the light of the sonic screwdriver between the Angels, they continued their advance, their arms reaching forward, forcing him to back away. And because the rest of the hall was in complete darkness, he had no way of knowing how long he had left before he backed himself into a wall.

'OK, I'm getting that you're not happy,' said the Doctor placatingly. 'But can't we sit down and discuss this like reasonable people? Cup of tea, jammy dodgers, comfy chairs?' The Angels did not respond. Their eyes remained blank. Their jaws remained open. 'Look. I can—'

The Doctor slipped on the marble floor, lost his balance and landed heavily on his back. For a moment he found himself in total darkness, until he remembered he still had his sonic screwdriver in his hand. In one movement, he activated it and swung it upwards.

Its green glow illuminated the faces of the six Weeping Angels, all looking down at him with expressions of pure malice. They had him surrounded.

'Ah now, you've made a mistake, you see,' said the Doctor. 'Because I can see all of you at once. So the question now is... which one of us will blink first?'

As they reached the museum entrance, Amy grabbed the security guard, the same guard who they'd spoken to in the tunnel. 'You've got to turn the lights back on!'

He shrugged quizzically. 'I did not turn out lights.'

'Well somebody did!' yelled Amy. 'There's still somebody in there. In the dark!'

The security guard snorted and walked slowly over to a switchboard. Rory and Mark caught up with Amy, Mark red-faced with the exertion, Rory wearing his usual worried expression.

'Hurry up!' urged Amy.

The security guard made a 'tch' noise then flicked down a succession of switches. The hallway behind them flickered into yellow light.

'Thank you,' said Amy, muttering under her breath, 'at last.' With the security guard leading the way, they hurried back through the brightly lit museum.

Returning to the hall with the statues of mythical figures, they discovered the Doctor lying on the floor, the Weeping Angels encircling him, locked in position as they prepared to strike.

'Doctor!' Amy rushed over to him and helped him slide out from beneath the scrum of Weeping Angels.

'I've been trying not to blink for the last minute,' said the Doctor. 'Harder than you'd think.' While Rory and Mark kept a careful watch on the Angels, the Doctor brushed himself down, straightened his jacket and tie, and approached the security guard.

'Hello.' The Doctor put a friendly arm around the guard's shoulders. 'You're probably wondering where those six new statues have come from.'

The guard nodded dumbly.

'Well, I shouldn't worry about them if I were you, they won't be here in the morning,' said the Doctor. 'But until we're all safely out of the building, let's not let them out of our sight, eh?'

Mark coughed to get the Doctor's attention.

'Oh,' said the Doctor, remembering. 'But first you might like to pop down to the Tabularium. I think there might be two people locked in down there...'

12 August 1998

Mark lay in bed, woken by the morning sunshine. He pulled on his glasses and the rest of the room fell into focus. The pillow from the centre of the bed lay on the floor where he'd thrown it the night before.

Rebecca perched on the balcony in a summer dress, gazing out into the street whilst thumbing through her copy of *The Beach*.

'Rebecca?' said Mark.

'Oh, you're awake now, are you?' she said, putting down her book. The morning sun shone in her hair like a halo and gave her skin a golden glow.

'About last night.'

'Yeah?'

Mark swallowed. 'Just checking. It wasn't another mistake, was it? Another "one-off"?'

Rebecca raised an eyebrow. 'Is that what you want it to be?'

'No, no, I don't,' said Mark hurriedly.

'Me neither,' said Rebecca. 'In fact, I hope it's going to turn out to be the complete opposite.'

Mark climbed out of bed, his feet slapping on the tiled floor. He wanted to rush over and kiss Rebecca, but looking at her sitting in the window, he changed his mind. 'Wait there.'

'What?'

Mark picked up his camera and focused on Rebecca. 'Hold on, don't move, I just want to capture this moment.' As she turned to gaze out into the street with her impossibly blue eyes, he pressed the button and the camera shutter clicked.

Chapter 10

29 October 1999

Now 42 years old, Mark paused outside the office block and gazed up at the familiar concrete facade. This was where he'd worked for over ten years, starting out as a junior assistant, gradually taking on more and more responsibilities until eventually they'd made him a partner. Or rather, this was where his younger self would be working for the *next* ten years.

The reception area was just as he remembered; OK, so the walls were a different colour, and the sign above the desk read 'Pollard & Boyce', but Ron sat at the desk leafing through a copy of the *Daily Mirror* as usual. The only difference was that he now had a full head of hair.

Mark approached the desk. 'Harold Jones to see Mr Pollard, five o'clock.'

Ron nodded and informed the relevant office on the phone. 'They're sending someone down.'

A minute later, the internal door opened and Siobhan emerged.

'Mr Jones, nice to meet you at last,' she said, shaking his hand.

Mark couldn't help but smile. Siobhan was still in her early thirties, bright-eyed and fresh-faced.

Siobhan took him up the stairs to Pollard's office. Mark caught a glimpse of his reflection in the glass door. He'd taken great care not to look like his younger self. He'd grown a beard, dyed his remaining hair black and, as a finishing touch, wore a pair of tinted sunglasses.

Although he'd spoken to Frank Pollard on the phone numerous times, this would be the first time they'd met in person. Over the last year Mark had divided his time between New York and Edinburgh but now he'd decided to move to London, and had purchased a flat in Highgate. He wanted to be nearer to his younger self. Oh, he wouldn't try to speak to him or anything like that, but it wouldn't hurt to keep an eye on his progress, from afar. And, more than anything else, Mark longed to see Rebecca again.

'Mr Pollard is ready for you.'

Mark discovered Frank Pollard at his desk, beaming with pride. Even he looked younger than Mark remembered, his cheeks plump and ruddy with health.

'Harold, Harold,' said Frank. 'Overjoyed to finally make your acquaintance, in the flesh, as it were.'

'You too,' said Mark, taking a seat. 'I would've visited earlier, but my business keeps me out of the country.'

'Understand entirely.' Frank helped himself to a boiled sweet. 'Why visit Croydon when you could be basking in the manifold delights of "the big apple", so to speak? Can I get Siobhan to make you anything? Coffee? Tea?'

'No, I'm fine thanks. You're probably wondering why I've come to see you.'

'I must confess to being a little intrigued. Your last "electronic mail" was most mysterious.'

'I'm here to ask a favour.'

'A favour?' Frank leaned forward onto his desk. 'And what variety of favour might that be?'

'I believe you've recently advertised a vacancy, for a junior assistant.'

'We have.'

'But you haven't filled the position yet?'

'We have not, as yet. We have whittled the candidates down to a shortlist, as it were.'

'I was wondering if I might make a suggestion. A recommendation. You see, I'm, er, *acquainted* with one of the applicants, and would be extremely grateful if you'd consider giving them the position.'

'Hmm. That is quite a favour to ask.'

'I realise that.'

'May I ask the name of this person with whom you are, shall we say, acquainted?'

'Mark Whitaker.'

Frank opened a file on his desk and skimmed through the papers. 'Mark Whitaker. Mark... Whitaker. Ah, here he is. We interviewed him earlier this week. A personable enough young man, if a little lacking in confidence, but not really in the same league as the other candidates.'

'But I think if you were to give him a chance, he'd prove himself more than capable.'

'Hmm,' said Frank, inspecting the application. 'I *suppose* he may have *potential*.'

'Look, I'm not asking you to take on someone who can't do the job. I'm just asking you to take him on for a trial period. If it doesn't work out, then you're free to get rid of him. And I'm not suggesting you do him any special favours. Treat him exactly as you would any other member of staff. And in return I'll continue to put as much business your way as I can.'

'This is most unorthodox. But bearing in mind how highly we regard you here at Pollard & Boyce, it would be injudicious, if not unprofessional, of us to overlook such a… glowing character reference.'

'So you'll give him the job?'

'Yes. For a *trial period*.' Frank made a note on Mark's application with a dramatic flourish.

'There's one other thing.'

'Yes?'

'My involvement in this has to remain confidential. As far as Mark Whitaker is concerned, he got this job entirely on merit.'

'I *see*.'

'You mustn't mention my name to him. It's vitally important he never finds out about this.'

'Discretion is, of course, assured,' said Frank. 'This lad, is he a relative of yours?'

'Something like that. Let's just say I have great expectations for him.'

'With you cast in the role of Magwitch?' chuckled

Frank. 'Was there anything else?

'No. That's everything.' Mark made his farewells and left, having ticked one more item off the list.

31 October 1999

'No milk I'm afraid,' said Mark, handing Rebecca a mug of tea. She was too tired to care. Her back ached, her fingers ached, her feet ached. But at least it was all over.

Well, the actual *moving* part of the move was over. In terms of furniture, all their new front room had to offer was a battered leathered sofa, an Ikea chair and Mark's portable television. Cardboard boxes filled the floor, piled four high, leaving only a narrow route from the sofa to the door. They'd all have to be unpacked, but that could wait. For now, Rebecca just wanted it to be over.

Oh, it was exciting. Not just moving to London's glamorous Camberwell, but moving in with Mark. It made things official in some way. For the last year they'd basically been living together anyway, but then she'd got the job at Imperial College, so since September she'd been sleeping on a futon at Lucy and Emma's, with Mark coming down at the weekends to go flat-hunting.

And now here they finally were. Drinking black tea in their own flat. Rebecca leaned back in her chair as she watched Mark fiddle with the aerial. It was the last episode in the second series of *Cold Feet*, and it was vitally important they didn't miss it.

Mark's mobile phone bleeped. 'Hello, yes? ... Yes,

that's right.' He winced apologetically to Rebecca. 'No, it's fine, I wasn't in the middle of anything. Um...' He fell silent as the person on the other end of the line spoke for several minutes. 'Thanks. Thanks for letting me know... Yes, and you too. Goodbye.' He switched off the phone and looked at Rebecca.

'What was that?'

'I got it,' Mark replied at last. 'I got the junior assistant job, with Pollard & Boyce.'

'You *got it*?'

'I'm on a trial period for the first three months, but... yes.' Mark sounded like he could hardly believe his good fortune. 'I start on the eighth.'

Despite all her aches, Rebecca hauled herself off the sofa and hugged him. 'I knew it, I *knew* they'd take you on. What did I tell you? Oh ye of little faith. Well now we have a *second* reason to celebrate!' Rebecca headed into the kitchen and opened the fridge. It was empty apart from the bottle of champagne she'd placed there earlier. She couldn't find any glasses so she rinsed out a couple of chipped mugs before returning to the living room. 'Champagne in mugs, I'm afraid. Truly we live the life of decadence.'

'Start as you mean to go on,' observed Mark drily.

Rebecca peeled off her jumper, wrapped it around the bottleneck and popped the cork. Then she chugged the wine into the mugs and passed one to Mark. 'There you go,' she said, lifting her mug. 'To our new flat, and your new career as a top-flight city lawyer.'

'Hardly that,' said Mark. 'God. Our new flat! Moving in together.'

'Yeah. Serious stuff.' Rebecca sipped the champagne,

feeling the tickle of the bubbles on her tongue. 'All grown-up and everything.'

'We'll be getting married next,' said Mark light-heartedly.

Rebecca snorted with laughter. 'What?'

'Well, it is, isn't it? The next logical step.'

'Is this you proposing to me?'

'No,' said Mark. He took a small box out of his jacket pocket and knelt before Rebecca on one knee. He opened the box to reveal a glinting diamond ring. '*This* is me proposing to you.'

A section of the TARDIS console exploded in a shower of sparks. The floor jolted and shuddered, threatening to throw Amy to the ground. 'Doctor!' she yelled, holding on for dear life. 'What's happening?'

They'd only left Rome ten minutes earlier, and had barely taken off before the TARDIS had started making a warping, grinding noise and everything in the control room that wasn't fixed in place fell over.

'More wibbliness in the space-time continuum, right?' suggested Rory, picking himself up.

The Doctor danced around the console, flicking switches, his forehead furrowed in concentration. 'More wibbliness. Yes. The fourth of November. The year 2000.'

'Another one of the items on Mark's list?' suggested Amy.

'There wasn't an item on his list for November 2000.'

'But that means…' said Rory.

'It *means* our friend isn't behaving himself.' The

Doctor banged the console and whooped as it began to make the familiar materialisation sound. 'Trouble, here we come!'

Chapter 11

4 November 2000

Pressing her lips together to remove any excess lipstick, Rebecca studied her reflection in the mirror one last time, looking for flaws. She couldn't find any. Amanda, the beautician, stood behind her, smiling proudly. 'Oh, you look *perfect*.'

Rebecca checked her hair, which had been painstakingly curled into ringlets and pinned, then, as though balancing a book on her head, she stood up. She desperately wanted to take a deep breath, but the corset of her wedding dress wouldn't allow it. Everything had been squeezed and tightened for maximum effect.

She turned to look at Lucy and Emma in their identical, peach-coloured bridesmaid outfits. She'd rather enjoyed the idea of forcing Lucy into something feminine for once.

There was a knock at the door. 'Respectable?' called Rebecca's father.

'No, but come in anyway,' replied Rebecca. Her father walked in with an embarrassed smile, resplendent in his morning suit, and paused as he took in his daughter's transformation.

'My little girl,' he said. For a moment she thought he was going to say how proud he was of her, but in the way he was looking at her, there was no need. 'Feeling nervous?'

'No. I'll be glad when it's all over, though, if only because then people will stop asking me that. Because if there's one thing guaranteed to make you nervous, it's people asking you if you're nervous all the time.'

'I won't pay any attention to that,' said her father. 'That's just the nerves talking. The, um, cars are outside, if you're ready?'

'Here goes, then,' said Rebecca. Once again she wished she could take a deep breath. She turned to go, then halted in the doorway. 'Bouquet!' She grabbed the bunch of lilies from the dressing table. 'Would've been a complete disaster if I'd forgotten that.'

A harsh wind blew across the graveyard, whirling up the leaves as it went. Fearing it would damage his meticulously tousled hair, Mark retreated into the church porch.

Mark's task, along with his best man Gareth, had been to greet the wedding guests as they made their way up the path to the church. It had been very disconcerting to see his colleagues from work, his friends from university and his mates from the pub quiz all in their finest suits and dresses. It felt like he was starring in a romantic comedy.

'Wassup?' said Gareth, slapping Mark on the back. 'Still not too late to do a runner.'

'Very funny,' said Mark, wishing, not for the first time, that he'd chosen a different best man.

Gareth checked his watch. 'Twenty minutes. Time you were heading inside, just in case they get here early.'

'Yeah,' said Mark, rubbing the fingers of his right hand. They were beginning to tingle.

'Well?'

'He's here, Amy,' said the Doctor, absorbed in his wibble-detector. '*Somewhere.* Somewhere close and getting closer all the time.'

Amy brushed her hair out of her eyes. The TARDIS had brought them to Chichester, a well-preserved city with enough Georgian buildings, Roman walls and leafy parks to look picturesque; every other shop seemed to sell antiques or cream teas. Despite the gusty weather, the pavements bustled with shoppers, mostly families and slow-moving pensioners. It reminded Amy of Leadworth, but with more traffic.

The Doctor halted, spun on his heel, then ran back the way they'd come, bounding towards the cathedral, bounding like a gazelle with rubber legs. 'Quick!'

Amy and Rory exchanged glances and chased after him. The Doctor stopped again, shook the detector, then gawped at the approaching traffic. An SUV sped down the street towards them. It took Amy a few seconds to recognise the driver; it was Mark, his face half-hidden behind a beard and sunglasses.

'Stop!' yelled the Doctor, striding into the road in the

path of the car, his hands raised. The SUV screeched to a halt. This was followed by a second screech, a loud crash and the tinkle of broken glass as another vehicle slammed into the back of the SUV.

Old Mark emerged from the car, slamming the door angrily behind him. 'What the… what are *you* doing here?'

'I could ask you the same question,' said the Doctor. 'In fact, I *am* asking you the same question. What are you doing here?'

'Driving along quite happily until some maniac ran out in front of me.'

Amy studied Mark's face. He looked like he was hiding something. 'We're here because the Doctor detected wibbliness. Are you trying to make contact with your younger self?'

'No,' protested Mark. 'No, of course not.'

'Interesting,' said the Doctor. 'Because the wibble-detector never lies. Unless it's malfunctioning, which is always a possibility. But not in this case. I can feel the build-up of potential time energy. Makes all the hairs on the back of my neck stand on end. And tastes of *lemons*.'

'So where *were* you going?' asked Rory.

Before Mark could explain, the driver of the car behind him walked up to them. He was an overweight, colonel-ish man dressed in a chauffeur's regalia. Behind him Amy could see a limousine with shattered headlights and a crumpled bonnet.

'What the hell do you think you're playing at?' yelled the driver.

'I'm sorry,' said Mark. 'It wasn't my fault, this—'

The doors of the limousine opened and out stepped a man of 60 in a grey morning suit with neatly combed white hair, followed by the blonde girl Amy had seen in Rome, now impeccably made up and wearing a stylish bridal gown.

The bride marched towards them, huffing with the effort, holding her high-heeled shoes. 'I don't believe it. I don't *chuffing* believe it!'

'What? What's the matter?' the Doctor asked her, then his eyes widened. 'Wait! Are you getting married?'

'Of course I'm getting married! This is my wedding day! Or at least it was meant to be before it turned into an episode of the *Chuckle Brothers*.'

The Doctor took Mark to one side and whispered. 'Oh, no. You weren't. Your *own wedding*. The list you showed me, of all the times you could intervene in your past? *This wasn't on the list!* Do you know what you've done? You've gone off-list!'

'I wasn't going to *intervene*,' protested Mark. 'I only wanted to stand at the back and watch.'

'Stand at the back and watch?' The Doctor waggled his fingers in frustration. 'What have I told you? Paradoxes! Angels! *Ramifications!* Why do humans never do as they're told? Someone should replace you all with *robots*. No, on seconds thoughts, they shouldn't, bad idea.'

'Sorry to interrupt,' said Rebecca unapologetically. 'Did I just hear you say you were on your way to a wedding?'

'Yes, that's right,' said Mark. 'Saint Stephen's, in a village called Chilbury. It's for a couple, Mark Whitaker and Rebecca Coles...'

'But that... that's *my* wedding,' exclaimed Rebecca. 'You're on your way to *my* wedding?'

'*You're* Rebecca Coles?' said Mark, feigning surprise. 'What a coincidence!'

'Well, there we are, small world.' The Doctor clapped. 'So if, um, *Harold* here could move his car, you can be on your way, and get married, just as you should.'

'Not gonna happen.' The chauffeur shook his head, indicating the damaged limousine. 'Can't drive with it like this, the insurance won't cover it.'

'Oh, *fantastic*,' said the Doctor, slapping his palms on the bonnet of Mark's car. 'Fantastic!'

'Look,' said Mark. 'Since I'm going there anyway... maybe I could give you a lift?'

'A lift! It gets better!' cried the Doctor to the heavens.

'I don't suppose I have any choice,' said Rebecca. 'If I'm not going to be late.'

'Oh, I'm sure a small delay won't hurt,' said the Doctor hurriedly. 'Bride's prerogative. Make him sweat. What's fifteen minutes in the grand scheme of things?'

Mark took the Doctor, Amy and Rory to one side. 'But she *wasn't* late,' he said firmly.

'What?'

'She arrived bang on time.'

'Are you sure?'

'I remember my *own wedding*!'

The Doctor paused, weighing up the situation. 'Right! Everyone into... *Harold's* car. No time to lose, we have a wedding to attend! You're the father of the bride, I take it? Isn't she beautiful? I'd marry her myself, given half a chance! In you go!'

Mark opened the side doors of his car, and Rebecca and her father piled inside.

'Sorry, what are we doing?' said Rory. 'Isn't this changing history?'

'No. If Rebecca is late for her wedding, *that*'s changing history,' explained the Doctor. 'We have to get her to the church on time!'

'So, if you don't mind me asking, but who are you?' said Rebecca, her shoes in her lap. There was something strangely familiar about the four strangers. Particularly the guy in the driver's seat. Take away the beard and twenty years or so and he'd have been a dead ringer for Mark.

'A relative,' he said. He even *sounded* like Mark. 'On Aunt Margaret's side. From Canada.'

The young man to her right with the large nose and gormless expression groaned for no apparent reason. 'You're from *Canada*? All of you?' asked Rebecca.

'Yes.' said the guy in the driver's seat. 'A small place, about fifty miles north of Toronto. I'm Harold Jones, this is the Doctor, Amy, and Rory.'

Rebecca considered. Mark's mother had mentioned something about having relatives in Canada. It would explain the resemblance.

'You don't, um, sound very Canadian, if you don't mind me saying,' said Rebecca's father.

'No, but that's just it, you see,' said Amy. 'We Canadians often don't. It's one of the most interesting things *aboot* us.'

'So who exactly invited you to my wedding?' said Rebecca.

'We just happened to be in the country and Mark's mother invited us, as a last-minute thing,' said Harold. 'Not a problem, is it?'

'No. In fact, it's lucky you were here. Although, thinking about it, if you hadn't been here, I wouldn't have crashed into you in the first place.'

'Funny how things work out,' said the Doctor as the car came to a halt. At the junction ahead the traffic lights were on red. 'How are we doing for time, Mar – marvellous Harold?'

'Five minutes to one. We're not gonna make it. Not in this traffic.'

'Leave that to me.' The Doctor dug into his jacket and pulled out what appeared to be a large electric toothbrush. He leaned out of the window and aimed it at the traffic lights. It buzzed and in an instant the traffic lights turned to green.

'Well, what are you waiting for?' grinned the Doctor manically. 'Drive!'

Mark sat between his mother and Gareth on the front-row pew. The air in the church smelt of stone and furniture polish. He stared at his shoes, so shiny he could actually see his reflection. 'What time is it now?'

'Five minutes to,' said Gareth. 'God, I hope she hasn't done a runner.'

Mark's phone beeped. He had a message from Lucy and Emma, saying they'd been caught in traffic, but they'd be there in five minutes, followed by four exclamation marks and a smiley.

Mark's mother took his hand and she gave it a squeeze. 'Don't worry. She'll be here on time. I feel sure of it.'

Mark pulled up in the country lane outside the church, right behind Lucy and Emma's limousine. The Doctor, Amy and Rory jumped out of the car, instantly regretting it as they landed in deep puddles. Rory gallantly helped Rebecca onto the grass verge. 'Careful. It's seriously muddy out here.'

Mark couldn't take his eyes off Rebecca. She looked so *perfect*. How many times had he summoned up the memory of her on their wedding day? And now here she was, living and breathing, a memory made flesh. He'd even talked to her. Hearing her voice for the first time in fifteen years, seeing her so full of hope and excitement, Mark felt both an immeasurable joy and an immeasurable sadness. Every second he fought the urge to tell her who he really was and what would happen to her one night in April 2003. But that would have to wait.

He climbed out of the car to join them, taking care to avoid the puddles. How many times had he come to this church? Once to rehearse the wedding, once for the wedding itself, and then countless times to visit Rebecca's grave. From the roadside he could see the empty patch of grass where it would one day lie, in the shade of an old, gnarled yew tree.

Rebecca's father passed Rebecca her shoes and, leaning on the lychgate, she twisted her feet into them. 'All done. What time is it now?'

'Fifteen minutes past,' said her father, indicating the clock on the church tower. 'But don't worry, it's not as if they're going to start without you.'

'Fifteen minutes?' said Amy. 'But I thought...'

The Doctor licked a finger and held it to the air. 'History is shifting course,' he announced grimly as a blue light flashed across the gravestones. The same kind of light Mark had seen in Rome and the students' union. There was a tension in the air, like before a thunderstorm, and was it his imagination or was it getting dark?

'So you were telling the truth,' said the Doctor. 'She did arrive at the church on time.'

'What are you talking about?' said Rebecca. 'I'm only fifteen minutes late, it's not the end of the world.'

'I wouldn't be so sure of that.' The Doctor reached a decision. 'Desperate situations require desperate solutions. Wait here, all of you, I'll be back before you know it.' He clambered into the driving seat of Mark's car, revved the engine and accelerated into the road. Seconds later he disappeared from view.

'What does he think he's doing?' said Rory, flabbergasted. 'Thanks, Doctor, leaving us in the lurch outside the... church! Y'know, Amy, I think he's really flipped this time.'

'Look, you can stand here if you like, but I have a wedding to go to,' said Rebecca, taking her first determined steps toward the church. 'I think I've kept my future husband waiting long enough...'

'Wait!' said Mark. Rebecca paused. The leaves on the path swirled upwards as though caught in a gust of wind, and, with a grinding, whinnying sound, the

Doctor's blue police box appeared on the path directly in front of her.

The door creaked open and the Doctor emerged. 'Well, what are you waiting for? Get in!'

'What's going on?' said Rebecca, staring at the Doctor and his blue box in disbelief. 'What is that thing? And what is it doing here?'

'Just a short hop,' beamed the Doctor, patting the police box like it was an old friend. 'Same place, twenty minutes ago. Oh, and don't worry, there's plenty of room for all of us.'

'I'm sorry,' said Rebecca. 'Are you saying that's some sort of *vehicle*?'

'I assure you there's nothing to be scared of. Do I look like the sort of person who would kidnap a bride, on her wedding day, in a police box?'

'Yes.'

'It's all right,' Amy assured her. 'You can trust the Doctor.'

'But I'm *late* for my own wedding—'

'Just take a look inside,' said Rory. 'I mean, if you're already late, what difference does one more minute make?'

The Doctor stepped out of the way to let Rebecca see into the police box.

'But... but that's impossible,' stammered Rebecca in awe. 'It's like there's a whole *house* in there...'

Chapter 12

Mark, Rebecca and her father stepped into the TARDIS control room, looking around in awe.

'*This* is your transport?' said Mark.

Rory sympathised with them. It wasn't the easiest thing in the world, to step from the normal world into a time machine housed in another dimension. The Doctor's choice of decor didn't make it any easier; the centre of the chamber being taken up with a cross between an avant-garde brass sculpture and a child's activity centre.

The child in this case being the Doctor. He darted around the console, entirely in his element. Rory had a theory that at least half the buttons on the console didn't actually do anything and the Doctor only pressed them because they made an interesting noise.

'You know,' said Rebecca to her father. 'I don't think these people actually *are* Mark's relatives.'

Rebecca's father nodded. 'I wouldn't be surprised if they weren't from Canada at all.'

A grinding sound filled the chamber, the central column of the console came to a rest and the Doctor bounded down the steps to throw open the main doors. 'Here we are!'

Rory followed the Doctor, Amy, Rebecca and her father outside. The TARDIS had landed on the village green opposite the church. They'd moved about a dozen metres.

The Doctor checked the clock tower. 'Five minutes to one.' He grinned at Rebecca. 'A little bit early, but now you'll be able to make it to the church, bang on schedule.'

'Sorry? You're saying we've gone *back in time*?' asked Rebecca.

'Only a little bit,' said the Doctor, leaning casually against the TARDIS. 'It'll hardly notice.'

'Er, Doctor,' said Rory. 'Are you sure this isn't cheating?'

'No.' The Doctor looked offended. He straightened his tie. 'It's the opposite of cheating. It's enforcing the rules. That's what I do. That's my *thing*.' He clapped, then returned his attention to Rebecca and her father. 'Well, no time like the present, in you both go.'

Rebecca was about to cross the road when suddenly a heavy goods lorry thundered down the lane, its horn blaring. Rebecca stepped back onto the village green but, as the lorry passed by, its wheels sluiced up the puddles, splashing muddy water all over her dress.

Everybody waited until the lorry had gone before speaking. 'Whoops,' said Amy sympathetically. 'I'm sure it'll dry-clean off.'

Rebecca looked down at her mud-spattered skirt.

She breathed in as much as she could, and said, 'I'm *supposed* to be getting married! In *three minutes'* time!'

The Doctor took Mark to one side. 'I don't suppose, by any chance, when she turned up at the wedding she was like this, was she?'

Mark shook his head.

'Sort of thing you'd remember?'

Mark nodded.

'Right!' declared the Doctor. 'All of you, wait here, don't move an inch.' He ruffled his hair, then darted back into the TARDIS, slamming the door behind him. The lamp on the top of the police box flashed, and with a whirl of wind, it disappeared from view. Only to reappear a second later. The door swung open to reveal the Doctor holding up a brand-new wedding dress, identical to the one Rebecca was wearing.

'Took me a while to find the shop where you'd bought the dress and get them to run up an exact copy, but I got there in the end. Thinking about it, I really should've asked you which shop it was before I left. Ooh, that Samantha does go on, doesn't she? Anyway, there you go.' The Doctor offered Rebecca the dress. 'Problem?'

'Yeah, slightly,' said Rebecca through gritted teeth. 'Firstly, if you think I'm changing into it standing here in the road you've got another think coming.'

'Oh, I'm sure you've got nothing to be embarrassed about,' smiled the Doctor benignly. 'No. That came out sounding wrong. What I meant to say was, you're welcome to change in the TARDIS.' He held open the doors of the police box.

'And secondly, I'm supposed to be getting married

in *two minutes* and it took me *half an hour* to get laced up into this thing.'

'Half an *hour*?' The Doctor was aghast. 'Half an hour? Right! Back in you go.' He ushered Rebecca, still clasping her new wedding dress, back into the TARDIS. 'And you too, Amy, you know how women's clothes work.' A confused Amy followed them into the police box. Its lamp flashed and it vanished. And reappeared one moment later. The doors swung open to reveal Rebecca in her brand new, perfectly clean, wedding dress, Amy and the Doctor behind her.

The Doctor checked the road for traffic. 'OK. Safe to cross. Got everything?'

'I think so.' Rebecca turned to her father, who was regarding the proceedings with utter bafflement. 'My bouquet!' she remembered in horror. 'I left it in the limo!'

The Doctor took Mark to one side. 'And she had it at the wedding?'

'Yes,' said Mark. 'She threw it, Lucy caught it.'

'Right!' cried the Doctor in frustration, disappearing into the TARDIS. It vanished and reappeared. The Doctor emerged brandishing Rebecca's bunch of lilies. He thrust the bouquet into her hands. 'Anything *else*?'

Rebecca shook her head.

'Then let's get you *married*.' The Doctor led Rebecca, her father, Amy and Rory across the road. After they'd gone through the lychgate and were halfway up the path to the church, the Doctor stepped in front of Rebecca and her father, forcing them to stop. 'One last thing.'

'What?' said Rebecca.

The Doctor stared at Rebecca intently, touching her forehead with his fingers, and spoke in a steady, hypnotic tone. 'You will have no memory of this, of meeting me, Amy, Rory, or Harold. As far as you're concerned, you came here in your limousine, without incident.'

'We... we came here in our limousine,' Rebecca repeated hesitantly.

'Good, good,' said the Doctor. He then repeated the process with Rebecca's father.

'We came here in our limousine,' Rebecca's father confirmed.

'Excellent. Now, when I click my fingers, I want both of you to wake up, make your way into that church, and have the most wonderful day of your *lives*.' The Doctor clicked his fingers.

Rebecca twitched, blinking as though waking up. Then she saw her father beside her. He was looking around with a puzzled expression, then turned to her and said. 'Ready?'

Rebecca nodded, took her father's arm, and they headed up the path to the church.

Something wasn't quite right. As they reached the porch, Rebecca released her father's arm and glanced back at the graveyard, down the path to the road where four people stood by the gate. She couldn't see their faces, but one of them seemed to be dressed as an old-fashioned professor.

There was a squeal of tyres as a limousine pulled up outside. Lucy and Emma tumbled out in a flurry of skirts and swearing. They jiggled their shoes onto their feet and stumbled up the path towards her. 'Sorry,' said Lucy breathlessly. 'Traffic was literally insane.'

'You're here now, that's the main thing,' said Rebecca.

'I think it's time…' Rebecca's father gently reminded her, offering her his arm.

'Ready,' said Rebecca, taking one last look back at the graveyard. She'd been coming to this church ever since she was a little girl, and she'd never noticed how many statues of angels there were before.

Amy felt a warm glow as Rebecca, her father and her two peach-coloured bridesmaids disappeared into the church. Amy checked the clock. It was one o'clock exactly. They'd made it.

Mark began striding purposefully up the path to the church. 'Mark!' the Doctor shouted after him. 'Where do you think you're going?'

'I told you,' said Mark. 'To stand at the back and watch. It won't do any harm.'

'Won't do any harm?' snapped the Doctor. 'After *everything* I've told you, everything we've been through?'

'It won't do any harm, I know it.' Mark turned to continue up the path.

Two statues blocked his way. Two statues of angels, standing solemnly in front of the church, their hands cupped beneath their faces, their eyes as blank as stone.

'The Angels,' gasped Amy. 'They were here all the time!'

'Attracted by the wibbliness,' explained Rory, for

his own benefit if no one else's.

'Mark!' shouted the Doctor. Mark was frozen to the spot in terror. Amy glanced away from him – to see four more statues in the graveyard, one crouched by a tomb, lowering its hands, one emerging from behind a grave, the other two rising from either side of a war memorial.

The Angels were too spread out for Amy to see them all at once. Trying her best not to blink, Amy turned to face the Angels by the church. They had moved closer to Mark, paused as they stalked towards him, hands raised above their heads, their fingers extended like claws.

Mark staggered backwards, tripping over his own feet. Amy dragged her eyes away from him to check on the other four Angels. They had advanced towards Mark as though to cut off any lines of escape, forcing him to retreat down the path towards the road.

'They're trying to *stop* him getting into the church,' said Amy. 'Why are they doing that, if they want him to cause a paradox?'

'Yeah,' said Rory sarcastically. 'That was my major concern too.'

The Doctor dashed up to Mark and grabbed him by the arm. 'Quick!' he said, dragging Mark away from the Angels. 'Amy, Rory, keep looking at them, try not to blink!' he shouted as he guided Mark back to the lychgate. Mark's eyes were wide with fear. He'd been scared out of his wits.

And then Amy realised she wasn't looking at the Angels. And nor was Rory. She spun back to see that four of the Angels had continued down the path towards them, their bodies contorted with anger, their mouths caught in silent screams. But if she could only see four of them, that meant there were two she couldn't see...

'Into the TARDIS!' ordered the Doctor. 'Fast as you can.' Amy didn't need telling twice. She sprinted through the lychgate, paused to check there was no traffic in the road, then splashed through the puddles to the TARDIS. Thankfully the Doctor had left the doors unlocked.

Rory, the Doctor and Mark hurried in after her. The Doctor bolted the door shut and darted over to the console. In seconds, the arduous groaning of the TARDIS take-off filled the air.

'They were *waiting* for us,' said Amy, her voice hoarse with fear. 'They were *expecting* us to be there...'

Gareth tapped his spoon on his glass. 'Groom's speech!'

Mark took one last sip of his water and stood up in front of everyone he knew.

The function room of the Grand Hotel fell silent. All of Mark's friends were there: Emma and Lucy, actually wearing dresses; Rajeev, flown over specially; Gareth, who had turned out to have unexpected depths; Siobhan from work, at a table with Mr Pollard and Mr Boyce, the two solicitors trying to outdo each other with the size of their buttonholes; Rebecca's parents, giving him approving, encouraging looks. And to his left, his mother, smiling for the first time in ages. And finally, to his right, Rebecca. His wife. Looking more elegant and glamorous than he'd ever dreamed possible.

Mark's hand trembled so much he could barely hold onto his speech. On top of that, his hand had started tingling again, like he was holding a battery. The feeling had been coming and going all day.

'Hello,' said Mark nervously. 'I've just got married. I'm a happily married man.'

There was a ripple of encouraging laughter.

'This'll be a short speech, you'll be glad to hear, because I'm sure we're all dying to find out why Gareth has set up a slide projector. But, as is traditional, I have to thank a few people.

'Firstly, I should thank my best man, Gareth, for his unwavering support and for his generous offer of a one-way ticket to New Zealand ten minutes before the wedding. I think he was joking. I *hope* he was joking. I'd also like to thank him for organising such a magnificent stag do, because unfortunately I didn't get a chance to thank him at the time due to an unexpected bout of food poisoning.

'I'd also like to thank the bridesmaids, Emma and Lucy, for making sure that Rebecca turned up, for which I will be eternally both surprised and grateful. And I'd like to thank Rebecca's parents, Olivia and Rodney, and my mother, Emily, for all their help. This day is a tribute to their kindness and generosity.

'Before I go any further, there's one more person I should mention. The person who sadly couldn't be here, who I wish was here more than anything else in the world, but who I know who is here in spirit, and that's my father, Patrick. I miss you, Dad.'

Mark paused. He could feel tears forming in his eyes. Because as he'd said those last words, it was like hearing the news of his father's death all over again, thinking of all the things he'd never get to tell him.

Looking across the room, at all the familiar faces lit up in the glow of the chandeliers, something drew Mark' gaze to the far end of the function room where a set of double doors opened onto a stairway. The doors should've been closed for his speech, but instead they were open. There was a man in the doorway, watching him. A man who looked just like his dad.

Mark glanced at his speech, then looked up. The man had gone and the doors at the far end of the function room were closed.

Mark cleared his throat. 'And finally I'd like to thank Rebecca, for everything, basically. For being my best friend, ever since I've known her. For always being there for me. For being a constant source of warmth, of inspiration, of laughter. And for doing me the very great honour of agreeing to be my wife.' He lifted his glass. 'To Rebecca.'

The night had turned cold, so they weren't likely to be disturbed in the hotel garden. The picnic tables were still wet from the rain, as Rory had discovered when he'd tried sitting on one. They were also unlikely to be seen, as the only light came from the windows of the TARDIS, parked unobtrusively in the corner, and the windows of the hotel as they flashed in time to the muffled strains of 'Dancin' In The Moonlight'.

Rory couldn't help searching the darkness for signs of a Weeping Angel. The Doctor had assured him that the moment of crisis had passed, and the Angels would now be in hiding, conserving their strength. That's why the Doctor had permitted Mark to watch his younger self delivering his wedding speech.

The Doctor gazed into the night, hands in his pockets, looking like he had all the troubles of the universe of his shoulders. 'Everything I've told you so far has been wrong.'

'What?' said Rory.

'The Angels. They haven't been following Mark in the hope of him creating a time paradox.'

'What?' said Amy. 'But they're attracted by the wibbliness, you said, like moths to a flame.'

'Yes,' said the Doctor. 'But not because they wanted him to change his past, but because they wanted to ensure that he *didn't*.'

'Eh?' said Rory. 'But I thought you said—'

'Think about it. When we met them at the students' union, they were trying to keep the two Marks *apart*. The same when we encountered them again in Rome. The same again today.'

'But why?' said Amy. 'Why do that?'

'Because they're working to a plan. Something big. Something much, much bigger than Mark just bumping into his younger self.'

'Like what?' said Mark.

The Doctor didn't reply. Instead, he looked at Mark with all the sadness of his nine hundred years. 'You tell me, Mark Whitaker. You tell me.'

'I don't know. Honestly, I don't.'

'I let you see your wedding speech,' said the Doctor. 'But that has to be the last time. From now on, steer clear of your past.'

'Don't worry,' said Mark. 'After what happened

today, if you think I'm going anywhere near my younger self again, you're very much mistaken.'

'Good,' said the Doctor, opening the TARDIS doors. 'Because if you *do* try anything, the Angels will be waiting for you.'

Chapter 13

5 June 2001

Mark went to the bookcase, slid aside the *Harry Potter* first editions and unlocked the small wall-safe behind them. He slid out the battered envelope with *MARK WHITAKER, 7/10/2011* written on the front. Crossing to his desk, he took out the letter from his future self, with its list of occasions where he must intervene in his own past. A list which he'd now completed.

Mark took a sip of freshly brewed coffee, tore a sheet of paper from a pad, placed it beside the letter from his future self, and began to copy it out, word for word, line by line.

This wasn't the first copy he'd made of the letter. He'd made a copy back in 1998, the copy he'd shown to the Doctor in Rome, which he'd shredded on his return. The one where he'd deliberately not included the final part of the message:

But make sure you follow these instructions, Mark.

Because if you do, remember this:

YOU CAN SAVE HER.

Just as I did.

Yours sincerely,

Mark Whitaker, April 2003.

How many times had he read those words? Even reading them now for the hundredth time, Mark felt an ache in his heart. Rebecca need not die. It was written there in black and white, in his own handwriting.

He'd give anything just to speak to her again. Oh, he'd spoken to her at the wedding, but then he'd been pretending to be someone else. He wanted to talk to her as himself, to tell her how he felt. He longed to be with her, to hear her laugh, to hear what she thought of all the things she'd missed out on; all the films that had come out after her death, all the Christmases, Lucy and Emma's civil ceremony and their baby daughter. They had always said they'd go back to Rome for their tenth wedding anniversary. Now they could do that and so much more.

Slowly and meticulously, Mark copied out the letter. With each line, he'd pause to check that he'd reproduced the details exactly. Glancing back at the original letter, he found that the handwriting matched. There was no way of telling the two letters apart; because, of course, they were the same letter.

Mark was about to copy out *Because if you do* when he paused to glance out of the window. His reflection gazed back, a ghost suspended over a panorama of London. He could see the skyscrapers of the city, shimmering like the towers of a magical kingdom under the wine-red sunset. He could even make out the London Eye on the horizon, shining electric blue.

By now Mark was, more or less, a multi-millionaire. This flat had been his only indulgence; a penthouse at the top of an exclusive development. All the furnishings were modern and sleek, and one entire side of the lounge consisted of a window looking out across Parliament Hill.

But spectacular views and luxury flats didn't take away the pain. Mark returned to his work, and the words *YOU CAN SAVE HER*.

Everything else in the letter had come true, so why did he doubt this part? Maybe it was because it was too good to be true. But also because the Doctor had warned him that he must not change history, no matter what. Saving Rebecca would certainly count as changing history. But if he was destined to save her, as the letter claimed, then surely if he *didn't* save her, that would count as changing history too.

Mark put down his pen. He would leave the rest of the letter blank until after he had saved Rebecca. Then, and only then, would he fill in the rest. That way he could be sure the message was true. And if it meant he was changing history then so be it.

Mark looked out across London. His younger self would be somewhere out there. Mark wondered what he was doing right now.

Mark's younger self was working late in his office. Everyone else had left hours ago, while Mark remained behind to prepare for a case that had unexpectedly been brought forward.

He rubbed his eyes and thought of home. Rebecca would be home by now. Mark was rarely home before ten o'clock these days. They only saw each other for half an hour before bed, when they were both too exhausted to do anything but watch television, and for half an hour in the morning when they were in too much of a hurry to talk.

But it would all be worth it. He'd been promoted to senior assistant, and in a few years he'd be in line for junior partner. Then they'd be able to afford a place of their own and could start thinking about children. But in the meantime he had to make himself invaluable, which meant volunteering to step in whenever there was a crisis. Like tonight.

Mark sifted through the case notes. The case was similar to one they'd handled the previous year, Jones versus Maxwell, and it would be quicker to see what precedents they'd used then than to start from scratch. Mark finished his instant coffee and headed into Mr Pollard's office, the neon light flickering as he switched it on.

Mark opened the filing cabinet, slid out the Jones folder and returned with it to his desk. Then he opened it, expecting to find a sheaf of notes. Instead there was a second, slimmer folder upon which was written: *IMPORTANT: NOT FOR THE ATTENTION OF MARK WHITAKER.*

Mark checked the name on the folder. It read *Harold Jones*. Someone had accidentally misfiled the wrong folder. But who was Harold Jones? And why would his folder contain something that he was forbidden to see? He'd never even heard the guy's name before. Which was odd, because Mark thought he knew the names of all of their regular clients, and going by the thickness of this folder, Harold Jones was a regular client.

Mark considered putting the folder back in the cabinet. That would be the right thing to do. If he was forbidden from reading this file, there had to be a very good reason for it. But for the life of him, Mark couldn't think what it might be.

There was only one way to find out. If there was something Pollard or Boyce didn't want him to see, Mark wanted to know what it was. He opened the folder. The first thing he saw was a copy of the CV he'd sent in when applying for the position of junior assistant. Then there was a page of notes in Pollard's handwriting under the heading *PROJECT MAGWITCH*.

Mark read the notes, at first intrigued, then with a growing sense of indignation. It turned out that this Harold Jones person was one of the firm's most lucrative clients, who had personally intervened to make sure Mark had been given the job of junior assistant back in 1999. In return, Jones would continue to use Pollard & Boyce to handle his business. It seemed that Jones's interests ranged from property development to TV production companies. Always as a sleeping partner, investing money through third parties in order to retain his anonymity, reaping the rewards by selling the shares at a profit or by receiving dividends and royalties.

Mark leafed through all the pages but could find no explanation as to why Harold Jones had intervened to get him the junior assistant job. Except for one note that Pollard had scrawled in the margin of one page:

Estranged relative?

Whoever this Harold Jones was, Mark had to speak to him. There was an address included in the folder, a block of flats in Highgate. Mark returned the folder to the filing cabinet, grabbed his jacket and ran downstairs, not bothering to say goodbye to Ron on reception. After climbing into his car, he rang Rebecca on his mobile.

'Hiya husband,' she answered, her voice distant but cheerful.

'Hi. Look, just to say—'

'There was a crisis at work and you're going to be late?'

'Something like that, yeah. Sorry.'

'No, don't apologise. I'll just order in a curry and watch *Big Brother* on my own.'

'Can you leave me some? I had to work through lunch.'

'Was there anything else? Only I'm in the bath and I'm making the phone all foamy.'

'No, that's all. I don't know how long this will take, so don't wait up or anything.'

'I'll do my best. Bye then. Love you.'

'Love you. Bye.'

Mark tossed his phone onto the passenger seat, twisted the ignition and drove across London to Highgate, his mind racing with unanswered questions. After an hour's drive, he pulled up outside the apartment block. He was surprised by how impressive the building was; a smooth edifice of steel and glass, lit by ground-level spotlights. It looked more like a modern art gallery than somewhere where people might actually live.

Mark checked the address one last time. Flat 4-A. He headed over to the entrance and buzzed the intercom.

After about ten seconds, a voice answered 'Hello?'

'Hello. Harold Jones?'

'Yes. Who's this?'

'I'm from Pollard & Boyce. Urgent business.'

'Come up.' The security door buzzed. Mark swung it opened and stepped into the brightly lit reception area. The lift took him to the fifth floor, where a short corridor led to the panelled door for apartment 4-A. As he approached it, the door swung open.

'Hello?'

The man standing in the doorway looked oddly familiar. For a moment, Mark thought he was looking at his own father; the man had the same watery eyes, the same thinning hairline. But this man wasn't his father, he was only in his mid-forties at most. It was the weirdest thing. It was like he was looking into a mirror and seeing his future self staring back.

'More wibbliness?' prompted Rory.

The Doctor nodded. 'A build-up of potential time energy, the biggest one yet.' He strained his eyes at the surrounding parkland. In the distance, the lights of London twinkled in the twilight. 'Mark must be interfering with his own past... irresponsible idiot!'

Amy emerged from the TARDIS, pulling on her jacket and handing Rory his. 'Any luck?'

Rory shook his head. They'd only left Mark outside the hotel about ten minutes earlier. Then the TARDIS had started wheezing like a steam engine giving birth, and the Doctor had gone into madman-in-charge-of-a-mixing-desk mode, all wild eyes and twitching fingers.

'Where are we, anyway?' said Rory. 'I mean, nice view.'

'Hampstead Heath.' The Doctor banged his palm on his wibble-detector. 'Brilliant. I can't get a fix, the signal's swamping the sensors...'

'So how are we going to find this paradox thing?' asked Amy.

Suddenly there was a flash. Rory shielded his eyes as blue lightning sizzled over a block of flats on the edge of the park. The lightning seemed to concentrate at the top of the building.

'I think we've found it,' said Rory. 'I'm no expert, but that looks like wibbliness to me...'

'You're Harold Jones?'

Mark nodded slowly. The man standing in his hallway was his younger self. It was like being confronted by an old photograph. A face he'd seen many times in the mirror, but so long ago.

'May I come in?' said Mark's younger self.

'You're from Pollard & Boyce?' said Mark.

'That's right, I work there. But I think you already know that.'

And then Mark realised the second thing that was wrong about his younger self visiting him. He had no memory of this taking place. When he'd worked at Pollard & Boyce, he'd never found out about Harold Jones. He'd certainly never gone to visit him.

'I think you'd better come in.' Mark conducted

his younger self into the lounge. As he did, he felt a tingling in his right hand and noticed that his younger self rubbed his right hand at the same time. He'd felt it too. And there was an odd metallic smell in the air, the smell of dodgems and Scalextric cars. The smell of static electricity.

'Can I offer you anything? Coffee, tea?'

'No, I'm good,' said Mark's younger self. 'Can we skip the small talk?'

'If you like,' said Mark, sitting at his desk. 'So how can I help you?'

'You can *help* me by telling me who the hell you are,' said Mark's younger self aggressively. 'And why the hell you've chosen to interfere in my life.'

Amy caught up with the Doctor and Rory at the entrance of the apartment block. They were both staring up at the top floor of the building, where blue lightning flickered over the steel and glass.

'We may be too late.' The Doctor tasted the air. 'It *feels* like we're already too late.'

'What do you mean, *feels*?'

'Time running off the rails. Forging new paths, new possibilities.'

Rory looked around them warily. 'Yeah, but surely if things were going wrong, the Weeping Angels would be here too, right? Like moths to a gong and all that?'

'Oh *great*,' said Amy. 'Thanks for reminding me.'

'Oh, they'll be here,' said the Doctor. 'You can be sure of that. They've probably been lying low in the cemetery down the road, awaiting their cue.' He aimed his sonic screwdriver at the door and it swung open.

'Amy, Rory. Stay here.'

'What?' protested Amy. 'Oh no. We're going with you.'

'Hey,' said Rory, grabbing the corner of Amy's coat. 'If the Doctor says we should wait here, maybe we should do as the man says. I mean, he does know what he's talking about.'

'Amy, listen to your husband,' said the Doctor. He ran into the brightly lit reception area and bounded up the stairs.

'Yeah. Like *that*'s ever gonna happen.' Amy sprinted into the reception area after the Doctor, her long-suffering husband trailing in her wake.

'You're a distant relative?'

'That's right,' said Harold Jones. 'On Aunt Margaret's side. I'm from, er, Canada.'

'Canada?' said Mark distrustfully. But the man's words had rung a bell. His mother had once mentioned a relative in Canada, a man who'd come to visit her once and who never replied to her letters or Christmas cards. And that *would* explain the resemblance…

'Did you visit my mum once, about six or seven years ago?' asked Mark.

'Yes. Yes, that's right. I happened to be in the country, for work, and I thought I'd look up some relatives.'

'Right,' said Mark. 'And that's why you got me the job at Pollard & Boyce?'

Harold nodded. 'Exactly. They handle a lot of my business, and so I thought I'd do you a favour.'

'You thought you'd do me a *favour*?'

'I recommended that they should take you on. But

only for a trial period, on the understanding that if you weren't good enough they were free to let you go.'

Mark remained unconvinced. 'Really?'

'So while I may have helped you get your foot in the door, everything you've achieved since has been entirely down to you.'

'They've been keeping you updated with my progress then, have they?'

'Something like that, yes. They call it Project Magwitch.'

As Rory reached for the door of flat 4-A, the Doctor yelled out from behind him. 'Wait!'

'What?' said Rory, his fingertips inches away from the door. A moment later, blue light began to flit intermittently across its surface, and across the walls, floor and ceiling of the corridor. Rory felt the hairs on the back of his hand stand on end. 'What is it?'

'A Blinovitch limitation field.' The Doctor levelled his sonic screwdriver at the door, gradually moving closer until there was a spit and crackle. 'Nasty stuff. Not good to get too close.'

'But can we get inside?' said Amy impatiently.

'In a moment...' said the Doctor, fiddling with his screwdriver. 'Nearly there, nearly there...'

While Harold explained about 'Project Magwitch', Mark took the opportunity to look around the flat, with its huge windows and its view over London, its designer chairs, its widescreen plasma television. A blue light flashed outside, like that of an ambulance.

Harold's story made sense, but Mark still didn't

believe it. 'And that's why you wouldn't let me handle any of your cases?'

'Exactly. I didn't want you to know. Look, I'm sorry. Maybe I should have told you, but—'

Harold kept talking but Mark had stopped listening. He'd noticed the two handwritten letters on Harold's desk, both of which included a list of places, times and dates going back to 1994. For 1995 he saw the details of an exam he'd taken at university. For 1997 he saw the address of a café in Coventry together with some lottery numbers. For 1998 it described the time he'd lost his wallet in Rome…

Mark suddenly remembered something Rebecca had once said to him a long time ago. About there being somebody at university who looked just like him.

'What are you doing?' cried Harold Jones as he realised, too late, that Mark was looking at the contents of his desk. He lunged forward in a desperate attempt to conceal the letters. 'You mustn't look at them, they're, they're *confidential*—'

Mark reached for one of the letters and, as he did, the fingers of his right hand came into contact with Harold's right hand. Mark heard a loud crackling sound, like a circuit being shorted, and an agonising bolt of pain shot up his arm. For a moment he had a sensation of cramp-like numbness, and could smell something burning, and then everything went black.

Chapter 14

The Doctor forced open the door to the flat and rushed in, Rory and Amy at his heels. The entrance hallway flickered with blue light, and smoke drifted in the air. It was like stepping into a night club. 'Hello?' the Doctor called out. 'Anyone home?'

They made their way through the smoke into a large room with a kitchen at one end and an office at the other. All the electrical appliances in the kitchen were going haywire, switching themselves on and off, with smoke pouring from their sockets. Blue lightning crackled across the floor, the ceiling, the walls and the large, wide window that took up one side of the room.

Rory's eyes started to stream from the smoke. 'What's going on?' he coughed. 'This place is going bonkers...'

'Time-energy discharge,' answered the Doctor, advancing into the room like a prowling tiger. 'Overloads the electrics.'

The light fittings fizzled, sending out cascades of

smouldering sparks. 'And what could have caused that?' said Rory.

tap-tap-tap

'I think I know.' Amy pointed towards the office, where two men lay slumped unconscious, one on the floor, the other across the desk. They both had their right arms outstretched and appeared to be giving off steam.

'Mark Whitaker, A and B.' The Doctor approached the bodies. 'Must've made physical contact, shorted out the differential.' He crouched beside the body of young Mark and took his pulse, before repeating the process with old Mark. 'They're lucky to be alive. It seems young Mark decided to pay his older self a visit.'

'So it wasn't old Mark interfering with his own past,' said Amy. 'It was young Mark interfering with his own *future*...'

tap-tap-tap

'But this shouldn't have happened?' said Rory. 'I mean, whichever way round it is, bumping into yourself's gotta be bad news, right?'

'It's not an ideal situation, no,' said the Doctor. 'We have to get them out of here. Rory, you take one Mark, I'll take the other.'

'Right,' said Rory, heaving young Mark into an upright position. While he did this, the Doctor managed to get old Mark standing and half-lifted, half-dragged him towards the doorway.

tap-tap-tap

Rory's lungs felt like they were on fire. As he struggled across the room with young Mark, all the light fittings burst into flames.

'I don't get it,' shouted Amy over the chaos. 'Why isn't the sprinkler system switching on?'

'Something's preventing it,' said the Doctor. 'Look.'

Rory followed the Doctor's gaze to the window on the far side of the room. Six stone figures stood on the other side of the glass, their hands pressed against its surface, staring inside with serene, blank faces. The Weeping Angels. All bathed in the flickering glow of the lightning.

'What are they doing?' shouted Rory to the Doctor.

'What do you think?' the Doctor yelled back. 'Feeding!'

But that was impossible, thought Rory. They were four storeys up. There was nothing for the Angels to be standing on.

tap-tap-tap

Rory couldn't keep his eyes on all of the Angels at once. Worse, with all the smoke swirling about, he could barely keep his eyes open. But that sound the Angels were making, they were tapping on the glass with their fingers…

There was a loud creaking, cracking sound. Rory caught a glimpse of the window covered in a spider's web of fracture lines emanating from the hand of one of the Angels. Then he had to blink, and an instant later there was an ear-splitting crash as the entire window shattered into a hundred pieces. The night wind roared in, fanning the flames higher and blowing the smoke towards Rory, Amy and the Doctor.

And Rory could see the Weeping Angels, never visibly moving but in the process of clambering into the room, one by one, their mouths wide as though screaming in triumph.

'Come on,' yelled the Doctor into Rory's ear. 'We have to go!'

Rory gripped young Mark by the waistband and tugged him into the hallway, through billowing smoke and surging, snapping flames. It was like they were escaping from hell itself.

Mark's older self came to with a retching cough. His eyes and throat stung and there was a smoky, acrid taste on his tongue. But he could smell fresh air and hear the rustle of leaves in the breeze. He was lying on the ground, he realised. Rory knelt beside him, taking his pulse. Behind Rory he could make out the Doctor and Amy, looking down at someone else laid out on the pavement, someone he couldn't see.

Then it all came back to him. The visit from his younger self. He could picture him framed in the doorway. Mark gasped deeply and suddenly at the memory.

'It's all right,' said Rory soothingly. 'You're safe, mate. Me and the Doctor rescued you.'

'You *rescued* me?'

Rory indicated the top of the apartment block. The top floor was a blaze of flickering orange flame, oily black smoke scudding up into the night sky.

'What... what happened?' said Mark, pulling himself to his feet.

'Hey, take it easy,' said Rory. 'You, um, seem to have bumped into yourself.'

Mark staggered over to the Doctor and Amy. They

were tending to his younger self, who had been put in the recovery position, his suit charred, his skin smudged with soot. For one horrible moment, Mark thought that his younger self might be dead, until he groaned and breathed in a deep, sleepy breath.

Mark stared at him, then up at his burning apartment, unable to take it all in. There was something else, something he'd forgotten. 'What did you just say?' he shouted at Rory. 'I *bumped into myself*?'

'The Doctor thinks you may have, er, made physical contact, or something. Which released a load of time energy.'

Physical contact? He could remember sitting at his desk, his younger self in front of him, and he could remember realising that his younger self hadn't been listening to him because—

'*The letter!*' breathed Mark. 'The letter I have to send to myself…'

'What?' said Rory.

'Where is it? Did you bring it here?'

'No. Should we have done?'

'Oh no,' said Mark. 'Oh no….' He looked at Rory, whose mouth hung open with incomprehension, then Mark turned and ran back to the entrance of the flats.

'Hey, where are you going? You'll get yourself killed!' Rory shouted after him. 'Doctor, the old one's doing a runner!'

Mark shoved open the security doors and raced up the stairwell, his chest straining with the effort. He passed some of the other residents of the block as they made their way downstairs. They called out to him, warning him not to go up there, but he ignored them.

He reached the fourth floor and slammed open the door to the corridor. A wall of searing heat hit him in the face, like he had just entered a furnace. He felt his skin prickle with sweat. The corridor ahead was clear, except for the thick black smoke that hung overhead like an indoor thundercloud.

Keeping his head low, Mark lurched down the corridor towards the door to his flat. His lungs felt like they were burning and he could hear his own ragged, desperate gasps for breath.

He made it through the door into his hallway. It was almost unrecognisable, lit a deep red by the pulsing glow of the fire. He could barely keep his eyes open. But he had to find the letter.

Mark entered his lounge to be confronted by a vision from a nightmare. The kitchen was a roaring mass of flames, a plume of fire stretched from his television up to the ceiling, and his sofa smouldered with foul-smelling smoke.

There were six figures in the room, standing perfectly still amidst the conflagration, each one holding its head in its hands, its wings folded back.

As Mark was forced to blink to clear his eyes of the smoke, the statues began to *move*. They slowly lowered their hands and turned to face towards Mark. There was no expression in their eyes. They seemed oblivious to the flames licking over their stonework.

Then, one by one, they opened their mouths, exposing their long, sharp fangs.

Mark stumbled blindly to his desk, feeling his way across the room until it banged into his midriff and the smoke cleared sufficiently for him to see the papers on his desk. As he watched, both the letters caught fire and shrivelled to black. The flames consumed both letters utterly, sending charred fragments fluttering up into the air.

Mark felt a hand on his shoulder. He turned.

'We have to go,' said the Doctor adamantly. '*Now.*'

Mark could see the Weeping Angels behind the Doctor, reaching out towards him. The sight caused Mark to freeze in terror. He couldn't speak or move.

The Doctor took him by the wrist and guided him back through the lounge, past the Angels and out into the hallway. Mark could hardly breathe and could barely see, but the Doctor kept leading him through the smoke and darkness, helping him down the stairwell and out into the clean night air.

Amy squealed with relief as the Doctor tumbled from the burning building, heaving old Mark with him. Old Mark's clothes and hair were dirty and charred, but he seemed otherwise unharmed. He sat on the pavement a few metres away from where his younger self was sleeping.

The residents of the apartment block had gathered in the car park, marvelling at the blaze as they awaited the arrival of the fire services. The fire would be visible all across London.

The Doctor squatted beside old Mark. 'What were you trying to do?'

'The letter, Doctor.' Mark took in another lungful of air. 'The letter I received from my future self, the one I had to send? It was in there. Both copies were in there!'

'Oh my God…' said Amy, her mouth falling open.

'I saw them burn,' said Mark wretchedly. 'So that's it. History's been changed.'

'What do you mean?' asked Rory.

'How can I have sent myself the letter, *when I don't have it any more!'* yelled Mark.

'Can't you just make another copy?'

'I can't remember every single word of the letter, can I? And if I got a single word wrong…'

'Oh. Right. Yeah.'

'Didn't you make any photocopies, or anything like that?' said Amy.

'No,' Mark replied, levelling his gaze accusingly at the Doctor. 'Because you told me *not* to, remember?'

The Doctor frowned. 'So, so now you can no longer send the letter to yourself, and the entire course of history has changed, with disastrous *ramifications* for the entire planet.'

He paused to straighten up, lick a finger and hold it in the air. 'Unless…' He reached for his wibble-detector, which was still slung around his neck, and began to urgently twiddle with its dials. 'Oh no. Oh no no no no no…'

'Unless?'

The Doctor didn't answer. He was too preoccupied taking a reading with the detector. Then he looked up at Amy with a fearful look in his eyes. 'Unless the course of history *hasn't* been changed.'

'What?'

'Which can only mean one thing,' said the Doctor gravely. *'Mark wasn't the one who wrote that letter!'*

'What? But of course he did,' said Amy. 'You said—'

'Of course,' said the Doctor. 'It was all part of their plan.'

'Whose plan?'

'The Weeping Angels.'

'Sorry, Doctor, you're saying the *Weeping Angels* wrote that letter?' said Rory. 'The one that Mark received in the year 2011?'

The Doctor nodded. 'A list of instructions that Mark would think came from his future self, in order to make sure he obeyed them to the letter. In order to make sure that I'd *tell him* to obey them to the letter.'

'But hang on, you're forgetting something. Mark said the letter was written in his own handwriting!'

The Doctor shook his head and turned to Mark. 'You never showed me the original letter, did you?'

'No,' said Mark.

'I wish you had,' said the Doctor. 'Because I would've noticed that it was written on *psychic paper*. Write a letter on psychic paper and the handwriting will look like that of whoever reads it.'

Mark pulled himself to his feet. 'But the name on the envelope was in my handwriting too.'

'Psychic envelope,' said the Doctor. 'Same material.'

'And the Weeping Angels got hold of all this *how*?' asked Rory. 'Did they just pop down the nearest psychic newsagents?'

'The Angels are creatures of perception. To them it would be child's play.' The Doctor looked at Mark mournfully, as though he was a condemned man. 'The copy of the letter you showed me. It wasn't the whole letter, was it?'

Mark twitched. 'What do you mean?'

'There was something else. Something else the Weeping Angels wanted you to do.'

'No.'

'What was the other part of the letter, Mark?' The Doctor exploded in anger. '*Tell me!*'

'There wasn't any other part of the letter, you saw the whole thing.'

'I don't think so. Because listen to me. Whatever was written in that letter, it's not true. The Angels wrote it, because they want you to *change history*. It is something that can *never happen*. Something *you must never do*.'

'No,' protested Mark, doubling up in pain as though crushed. His chest was heaving and he kept swallowing, gasping, grimacing, as though trying to speak but unable to find the words. 'No, you're wrong,' he hissed at the Doctor. 'It can happen. I'm going to *make it* happen.'

'Mark, you can't, no matter how much—'

Mark straightened up and regarded the Doctor with cold, angry eyes; eyes filled with years of loneliness and grief. But instead of speaking, he turned away and strode towards the car park.

'Mark. Where are you going? *Stop*—'

Mark raised his key fob, aimed it at his SUV, and unlocked it with a beep. He climbed into the driving seat. The Doctor attempted to grab the car door, but he was too late; the car's engine growled into life, its headlights flashed on with blinding brightness, and it swung out into the road. Amy, Rory and the Doctor could only stand by uselessly as it accelerated into the night.

As the car disappeared from view, the wail of sirens grew louder until two fire engines and an ambulance appeared at the end of the road, illuminating everything with their flashing lights. Firemen clambered out, shouting instructions and craning their necks to assess the blaze.

Distracted by the firemen, it took a few moments for Amy to realise the Doctor wasn't with her. He and Rory had returned their attention to Mark's younger self, who was still curled up on the pavement. He regained consciousness with a wheeze and splutter, his bloodshot eyes darting around in confusion. 'Who are you? What happened?'

'You came to see a man called Harold Jones,' said the Doctor calmly. 'Why?'

'Harold Jones?' Mark frowned as he struggled to remember. 'I was working late in the office, and came across this folder... he was the reason I got this job. And he had these letters on his desk, with lists of stuff from my life!'

'It's all right,' said the Doctor gently as he placed his fingers on Mark's forehead. Mark's eyelids drooped and his head lolled forward as he fell into a trance. 'You'll be fine. Listen to me. You will have no memory of the events of this evening.'

'No memory,' repeated Mark.

'The last thing you'll remember is working late in the office. You won't remember me, my friends or Harold Jones. When you awake, you will never have heard of him. Understand?'

Mark nodded.

'There was a small fire in your office, someone

dropped a lit match into a bin, you threw your jacket over it, that's how it got burnt.'

Mark nodded.

'And when you wake up, I want you to phone your wife and tell her you'll be coming home, then go back to your car and drive straight there. You've got all that?'

Mark nodded.

'Good.' The Doctor clicked his fingers.

Mark's head lifted. For a moment he looked around, not sure where he was, then he stood up. 'Sorry, um, excuse me...' he muttered, before speed-dialling a number on his mobile phone. 'Hiya... Yeah. It's me. Just calling to let you know I'm on my way home... Love you too.' Then, without registering the Doctor, Amy or Rory, he strolled over to one of the cars parked outside the building, got into it, and drove away.

The Doctor, Amy and Rory stepped aside as the firemen located the nearest hydrant and connected their hoses.

'So that's that?' asked Amy, rubbing the soot off her hands.

'I think so,' said the Doctor. 'Mark goes home to his wife, having forgotten all about tonight, and all about us...'

Rory's mouth fell open as a sudden, terrible realisation dawned on him. 'Wait a minute,' he said. 'Did you just say he's going home to his *wife*?'

'Yes—'

'But when I spoke to Mrs Levenson, she never mentioned anything about Mark being married!'

'No,' said Amy. 'And when I asked him a couple of days ago, he said he had no wife or children...'

'But we know he has a wife *now*, so if he doesn't have one in the future,' said Rory. 'Then that means either they get divorced, or...'

The Doctor suddenly looked incredibly old and gaunt. 'So that's it. That's what the Weeping Angels have been working towards.'

'You mean, something happened to Rebecca?' said Amy. 'Or rather, something's *going to* happen to Rebecca. Oh my God. She's going to die...'

'And Mark's going to try to stop it,' muttered the Doctor, staring into the depths of the night. 'He's going to try to save her.'

'But if he saved her,' said Rory, piecing it together. '... then he'd be changing history.'

'Not only that, but—' Before the Doctor could finish he was interrupted by a voice calling to them from down the street.

'Doctor! Amy!' A familiar figure ran out of the darkness towards them. As he got closer and slowed down, he moved into the glow of a street lamp and Amy could see his face.

It was Rory.

But Rory was standing right next to her, gawping in disbelief at the new arrival. Amy turned from him to the other Rory, the new Rory. He approached with an exhausted look on his face.

'Thank God,' he sighed in relief, rubbing his side and wincing. 'For a minute there, I thought I'd missed you.'

'*Rory?*' said the Doctor, regarding him suspiciously. 'What are you doing here?'

The new Rory give Amy a reassuring smile, before

he noticed his former self and his mouth fell open 'I'm, er, from the future, yeah?' the new Rory began. 'I mean, I was with you in the future, but then I was touched by an Angel…'

Chapter 15

21 April 2002

It had been their first major argument.

It all started when Mark suggested that Rebecca shouldn't bother to buy another car after her previous one had been written off. His point was that having a car in London was a waste of money, as she hardly ever used it except to go to her parents', and she'd said herself that driving in London was insanely stressful and dangerous.

Rebecca's response had been to accuse Mark of calling her a bad driver. Which hadn't been his point at all. It wasn't Rebecca's driving that worried him. It was everybody else's.

Rebecca had been driving to Peckham for the weekly shop when, as she turned left at a crossroads, the car on her right jumped the lights and crashed into her. She'd been lucky to escape with whiplash and a dislocated shoulder.

The argument happened the following night. They were both overtired, neither of them having slept more than a few hours since the accident. Mark still had the stress of the day coursing through his system, and Rebecca kept being woken up as her painkillers wore off. Then they had a day of dealing with the police, and the insurance. On top of that, they had to cancel their holiday in Paris which had been due to begin the following day.

That was what the final part of the argument had been about. Rebecca accused Mark of being glad that their holiday had been cancelled because it meant he could go back to work. Mark hotly denied this, but the problem was, Rebecca knew him too well. The thought of returning to work had occurred to him.

And that's why he spent the night on the sofa in the living room.

Rebecca woke as a jab of pain in her neck reminded her of her injury. Slowly and awkwardly, she eased herself into a sitting position and reached for the painkillers and water on the bedside table. She had to twist her waist to see what she was doing as she couldn't turn her head.

The alarm clock read *11:30*. The other side of the bed was empty. For a moment Rebecca thought nothing of it; she often woke after Mark had gone to work, until she remembered this was the first time she and Mark had spent the night apart since their wedding.

Rebecca washed and put on a fresh T-shirt, then headed downstairs, gripping the banister with her one good hand. She'd have a cup of tea and maybe watch the news. Today she should've been exploring the art galleries and museums of Paris with Mark; instead she'd be spending it alone in a cold flat.

Rebecca stopped at the foot of the stairs. She could hear something sizzling in the kitchen, and could smell the smoky aroma of pancakes. She wandered in to discover Mark at the oven with a frying pan in his hand, a string of garlic around his neck, a beret on his head, humming 'She' by Charles Aznavour.

'What are you doing?' said Rebecca.

'Making crêpes. This is my sixth attempt, I think I've almost got it.'

'I mean with the,' she indicated the garlic, 'and the,' she indicated the beret.

'Oh. Idea I had. For the next two weeks, I've designated this flat as French territory.'

'What?'

'If you can't go to Paris ... then let Paris come to you.' Mark slid the pancakes out of the frying pan and turned towards her.

'Please take that thing off, you look like Frank Spencer.'

'I thought it made me look like Che Guevara,' protested Mark. 'I got it while I was out shopping. Couldn't get snails or frog legs, but we have croissants, *pain au chocolat*, and later you have a choice of me attempting either *coq au vin* or ratatouille.'

Rebecca noticed the five bulging supermarket shopping bags on the side.

'I also thought,' continued Mark, 'that if we're going to be stuck in the flat together for two weeks, we might need some entertainment, so I got a few DVDs and videos.' Mark indicated one of the bags.

Rebecca rummaged through it. '*Amélie. Cyrano de Bergerac. Betty Blue. Mon Oncle. Asterix & Obelix Take On Caesar*. And the first two series of *'Allo 'Allo*...'

'Can't get more French than that.'

'Very true.' Rebecca sniffed the crêpes. 'So we're spending the next two weeks stuck in the flat together, are we?'

'I mean, I could always go into work, if you'd prefer, but I thought, two weeks with my gorgeous wife Rebecca, versus sitting in a solicitor's office in Croydon. No competition really.'

'Not when you put it like that. Is this your way of saying sorry?'

Mark handed her a pancake on a plate. 'Overdoing it, do you think?'

'A bit, yes.' Rebecca broke off some of the pancake and ate it. 'But I strongly approve.' She kissed him gently on the back of the neck. '*Merci beaucoup.*'

'You're lucky. I very nearly bought an accordion.'

'You have no idea how grateful I am that you didn't.'

'And you're sure you're OK with having me hanging around, waiting on you, hand and foot?'

'I could get used to it,' said Rebecca. 'I should get into car crashes more often. No, I think if I have to be stuck in the flat for two weeks, there isn't anyone in the world I'd rather be stuck with.'

'So you're not annoyed, about not going to Paris?'

'Not any more. I mean, it's not as if Paris is going anywhere. There's always next year.'

*

'Is this strictly necessary?' asked Rory as the Doctor ran the sonic screwdriver over him like a customs official with a metal detector. Instead of giving an answer, the Doctor darted across the control room and repeated the process with the other Rory, the Rory from the future.

It was a weird feeling to be in the same room as your future self. That person over there, with the surprisingly large nose and gormless face, would be him at some point. Staring back at his past self, who as far as Rory was concerned, was his current self. Which was confusing if you thought about it, so Rory decided to stop thinking about it.

'Completely necessary,' said the Doctor, closing his sonic screwdriver with a flourish. 'It's now safe for you both to be in the same room together.'

'Eh?'

The Doctor went into explanation mode. 'Blinovitch Limitation Effect. Two identical versions of the same person, at different points in their timeline, should not co-exist within the same space and time. All sorts of nasty potential for paradoxes. And if they should happen to make physical contact – bang!'

'Like with the two Marks?' said Amy.

'Like, as you say, with the two Marks,' said the Doctor. 'But I've now neutralised the effect. Ask me how.'

'How?' said the future Rory.

'You couldn't possibly begin to understand. But thanks for asking.'

Rory tried to get his head around it. 'So it's now safe for me to touch my future self?'

'Yes,' said the Doctor. 'Although I would strongly

advise you not to.'

'Why?' said Rory.

'Yeah, why not?' said the future Rory.

'Because it would look *odd*. Best keep your hands to, um, yourself.'

Rory and his future self exchanged indignant frowns. 'Right. Yeah. Thanks a lot, Doctor.'

'So where are you from?' Amy asked the future Rory with a flirtatious smirk. Rory couldn't help feeling jealous. 'What happened to you exactly?'

'Um, well, I'm not sure how much I can say,' said the future Rory hesitantly. 'You know, spoilers and stuff. But we were all in this field, on the South Downs, on the night of the tenth of April 2003, and the Weeping Angels were there too, and well, I got zapped.'

'Zapped?' said Rory.

'Back to 2001. Which was a bit of a head-scratcher, to say the least.'

'And then you came and found us?' asked the Doctor.

'Not *quite*. First I had to hang around for a month waiting for you to turn up.'

'What?'

'I was sent back to the first of *May*. Four weeks I've been stuck in the past waiting for you!' Future Rory sighed indignantly. 'I seem to spend half my life waiting for people!'

'Still, four weeks,' said the Doctor. 'Give you a chance to catch up on old times and stuff.'

'You try being dumped in the past with no money, no job, and nowhere to live! I could hardly go back to Leadworth, could I?'

'I'm sure you coped admirably. No need to go into the grisly details.'

'Hang on,' said Rory. 'If this is going to happen to me, I'd quite like to hear the grisly details, thank you very much. Give me some idea what I'm in for.'

'That's precisely why you mustn't know,' said the Doctor. 'And why your future self mustn't tell you. You've heard too much as it is.' He returned to future Rory. 'Let me get this straight. It was the night of the tenth of April 2003, when you were touched by the Angel?'

'Yeah.'

The Doctor swung the small monitor screen to face Rory. It showed the front page of a local newspaper. 'Which was the night that Rebecca Whitaker died.'

Future Rory nodded and swallowed. 'Yeah.'

'Right. Now, I need you to answer this as precisely as you can. When you were the Rory over there,' the Doctor indicated Rory, 'and your future self turned up, what did we do next?'

'What did we do next?'

'Yes. It's vitally important you remember.'

'I do, it's just that I'm not sure I should tell you. You know, spoilers.'

The Doctor let out an exasperated sigh. 'OK. Let me put it like this. I think the next thing I should do is that I should take us to the time and place where Rebecca was killed. If I were to do that, would I be changing history?'

'No,' said future Rory. 'That's exactly what I remember you doing last time.'

'Good. Then that is what we shall do.' He turned

to Rory. 'I hope you're paying attention to this, I'll be asking questions later.'

'Yeah, don't worry,' said Rory, tapping his forehead. 'Committing it all to memory.'

'Good.' The Doctor advanced on the console like a concert pianist about to give a recital, but before he could start laying in a course he paused. 'You know, it could potentially get a little confusing having two Rorys about the place...'

'I'm not confused,' said future Rory.

'No, me neither,' said Rory. 'I know which one I am.'

'Yeah, and so do I,' said his future self.

'Yes,' said the Doctor. 'But nevertheless it would be useful if *I* had some way of telling you apart.'

'What, like one of us growing a moustache?' said Rory.

'Yes, but there's hardly time for that, is there?' The Doctor bit his lip as he thought. 'Future Rory. Future Rory. "F" Rory. "F" Rory... Ha! I know! I have just the thing!' The Doctor jumped down into one of the storage areas by the interior doors, pulled out a chest, and rummaged inside it before extracting a red cylindrical hat with a tassel. 'Fez Rory!' the Doctor announced. He strode over to Rory and slid it on his head. 'Future Rory, Fez Rory!'

'Er, Doctor, I'm not the future one,' said Rory. He pointed towards his future self. 'He is.'

The Doctor snatched back the fez. 'You see, I *said* you'd start getting confused.' He bounded over to future Rory and placed it ceremonially onto his head. 'There. Now, you have to keep this on. The fate of the entire universe may depend on it.'

'Really?' said future Rory. 'The entire universe? Depends on me wearing a fez? That's how these things work, is it?'

'Now, if you'll give me a moment,' said the Doctor, returning to the controls. 'The sooner I get us to 2003, the sooner we can stop having two Rorys roaming about the place!'

Chapter 16

10 April 2003

At last, after nine years of waiting, the day had finally arrived. The day Rebecca died. Except this time everything would be different.

Mark drove through the narrow lane, squinting as the setting sun flashed through the hedges that towered over the road. In the distance he could see the black thunderclouds of the approaching storm. In an hour or so it would be pitch dark and bucketing with rain. But Mark would be ready. He'd left nothing to chance.

His mouth was dry with anticipation. He'd explored every option of how to prevent the accident. He'd considered simply stealing Rebecca's car, but what if a passing policeman caught him in the attempt? He'd spend the night in the cells while she continued to her death. No. He would have to keep it simple, intervening only at the last possible moment. Only then could he be sure he would prevent the accident without being part of the chain of events that led to it.

The details of the accident were indelibly burned into his memory. At 10.26 p.m., Rebecca was involved in a head-on collision with a heavy goods vehicle one mile from the village of Chilbury. She had just taken a blind left turn. The lorry was travelling at over fifty miles an hour. Because of the high hedgerows there was no way either of them could have seen the other. Mark had visited the site of the accident in preparation and knew every detail of the journey.

So all he had to do was to stop the lorry before it reached the fatal corner. Mark knew that the lane continued towards Chilbury, with no junctions or intersections, but about a quarter of a mile further on there lay a long stretch of road, the width of a single lane, that led uphill into the village. This was where the lorry had built up speed. This was where Mark's car would be blocking the road. The driver of the lorry would see it in plenty of time and be forced to come to a halt. And Rebecca, coming the other way, would also see the car and slow down. Only then would Mark move his car out of the way.

And then he'd have Rebecca again. All the years without her, all those long, lonely years of grief and regret, would be wiped out in an instant. They would never have happened. And if it summoned the Weeping Angels, then that was a small price to pay for the life of the woman he loved.

Almost without noticing it, Mark came to the point in the road where the accident had taken place. Would take place. Would no longer have taken place. He changed down gear, steered his SUV around the corner, and accelerated up the long, straight road to Chilbury. Then, at a small, gravelly lay-by about halfway up the road, he pulled in and switched off the engine.

He'd checked the area the week before. Even in torrential rain there was no chance of his car being stuck in mud. He'd checked the engine, there was no chance of it failing or running out of fuel. He'd checked the police report after the accident – read it so many times he knew it off by heart. In the ten minutes leading up to the accident, there had been no other traffic sighted on that stretch of road. At 10.16 p.m., he'd move his car into the lane, then he'd be able to watch from a nearby field as the lorry approached from a distance of half a mile. He'd thought of everything.

There was a rumble of thunder and rain spattered against the windscreen.

Rory followed the Doctor and Amy out of the TARDIS and immediately he flinched from the cold and hugged his coat for warmth. Thankfully his woollen chullo hat covered his ears, as the wind blasted icy rain into his cheeks. Beside him, Amy brushed her hair from across her face and pulled her hood over her head, while future Rory tried his best to look nonchalant whilst wearing an increasingly damp fez.

Only the Doctor seemed immune to the freezing weather. 'This is the place?'

Fez Rory nodded.

The Doctor handed them each a torch which they clicked on. The beams only extended a few metres into the gloom, the lights picking out an ever-shifting curtain of raindrops. Rory could make out uneven, mud-soaked turf beneath their feet. He'd have to be careful not to trip up.

'I'm getting wibbliness on an unprecedented scale,' said the Doctor as he took a reading from his wibble-detector. 'Hard to pinpoint the exact source, but this is it. This is the tipping-point, the moment where the future hangs in the balance.' There was a sudden boom of thunder and a flicker of bright blue lightning. 'The moment the Weeping Angels have been waiting for.'

'The dinner gong?' said Amy.

'With a big, juicy, space-time event on the menu. It's time for the *feast*.' The Doctor lowered his detector and clenched his jaw, his face filled with dread, then waved the beam of his torch downhill. 'This way, I think.'

As they followed the Doctor across the muddy field, Rory strained his eyes to see anything in the gloom. It was so dark he kept thinking he saw movement, but it was only his eyes playing tricks as they grew accustomed to the darkness. But then he saw it; a pale yellow light about a quarter of a mile away, at a point further down the hillside.

'There!' said Rory. The light came from inside a car parked halfway up a steep country lane.

'That must be him.' The Doctor turned to Fez Rory. 'Am I right?'

'Um, yeah. That's his car,' confirmed Fez Rory.

'Then there's no time to lose.' Using his torch to pick out the ground ahead, the Doctor strode towards the light with renewed urgency. 'But watch out. The Weeping Angels are here. And they will try to stop us.'

*

Ten minutes later, Rory's shoes were soaked through and his feet were numb. From here they could see that Mark's car had been abandoned in the middle of the road. Rory couldn't tell if the SUV's engine was running; all he could hear was the roar of the wind and the occasional crash of thunder.

'What's he doing?' said Amy. 'He's just left it there? Why?'

'His wife met her death on this stretch of road,' said the Doctor. 'A collision with an oncoming vehicle. Which can no longer *be* oncoming if there's a car in its way.'

'You got all that from just a parked car?' said Rory, stamping some feeling back into his feet.

'He's left the lights on, he wants it to be seen. It's a *warning*. Best way to stop a crash between two vehicles? Put something *large* and *very obvious* between them. It's what I'd do.'

'Er, Doctor,' said Fez Rory. He indicated a figure standing about twenty metres away, between them and the car. A man in a puffy winter coat, his face ruddy from the cold. He stared defiantly into the glare of their torches.

'Mark,' the Doctor shouted to him. 'Whatever it is you think you're doing, you have to stop!'

Mark shook his head. 'Whatever I *think* I'm doing?' he shouted. 'I'm going to save Rebecca. And there's nothing you can say or do that will stop me.'

The Doctor began to slowly venture toward him. 'After everything I've told you, haven't you learned anything? You have to move your car out of the way and let history take its course.'

'No.'

'You have to do it, Mark.' The Doctor wiped his hair, out of his eyes. His face and clothes were sopping wet, raindrops dripping off his nose and eyebrows. '*Listen* to me.'

'In about seven minutes' time a heavy goods lorry is going to come down that hill. If my car isn't there to stop it, that lorry will hit Rebecca's car. And I am not going to let that happen.'

'You don't have any choice!'

'But I do. Otherwise you wouldn't be here to try and talk me out of it,' said Mark, his face lit up by a flash of lightning. 'No. This time it's going to be different. This time she lives.' There was another boom of thunder.

'She *dies*, Mark. What has happened, has to happen. You can't change that.'

'Why not?' protested Mark. He began to back away from them, down towards the road.

'Because it's a *trap*,' shouted the Doctor, walking steadily towards Mark. 'Everything that's happened, it's all been engineered by the Weeping Angels to bring you to this point.'

For a moment it looked like Mark believed the Doctor, his face twitching as he fought back tears. 'They've given me the chance to save her,' he said, his chest heaving with rage.

'The Angels don't care if Rebecca lives or dies. They're just using her, and *you*, to give them what they want. A time paradox.'

'I don't believe you!'

'Then look around you, Mark!' shouted the Doctor. 'Look around you!'

The Doctor flashed his torch towards a marble-white figure stood in the pitch blackness five metres to Mark's left. The figure had its hands held out before it, palms upwards, the rain spattering and dribbling over its stone wings and Greek style dress.

The Doctor swung his torch to Mark's right, lighting up a second Weeping Angel in the same submissive posture.

Rory, Amy and Fez Rory flashed their torches around them, illuminating the wet grass, the shimmering sheets of rain, and four more Angels emerging from the void of darkness, two to their left, two to their right. All with their hands palms out before them, as though in greeting.

'Oh hell,' muttered Rory.

'You took the words right out of my mouth,' said Fez Rory.

'You brought them here,' said the Doctor with an edge in his voice. He took another step towards Mark. 'Just as I warned you not to.'

Mark backed away, his eyes darting between the Angels. 'No. No…'

'Don't worry,' the Doctor assured him. 'They won't stop *you*. They can't get involved directly, you see, they need the paradox to be the result of someone else's interference. But as for us… well, ha, that's another story.'

As the Doctor spoke, Rory kept moving his torchlight between the Angels. They were all still standing in the same posture, but was it his imagination or were they moving nearer? No. It wasn't his imagination. The four Angels to their left and right had closed in, to cut off any line of escape. 'Um, Doctor, about that...'

The Doctor ignored Rory, keeping his attention fixed on Mark. 'You think it's bad now?' he said. 'You have no idea what the consequences will be.'

'I know what I'm doing,' protested Mark, taking a stumbling step away from the Doctor. 'I'm going to save Rebecca.' Rory noticed that the Angels on either side of Mark had moved closer together. They were now only a couple of metres away from Mark, trying to get between him and the Doctor, to cut them off and prevent them from reaching the car.

'And you think that will make the world a better place?' said the Doctor.

'How could it be *worse*?' cried Mark. 'How could it? Answer me that! I've spent seventeen years without her. I don't care about paradoxes, I don't care about Angels.' Mark blinked back the tears forming in his eyes. 'I just want her back.'

'You can't have her back. She has to die.'

'Why?' screamed Mark. 'Why does *she* have to be the one who has to die?'

While the Doctor concentrated on Mark, Rory directed his torch into the blackness that surrounded them. With two Angels behind them, two to the sides and two in front, they were effectively caught in the centre of a circle.

The Doctor gave Mark a sympathetic smile, ignoring the two Angels who flanked him on either side. 'Why do you think the Angels chose you, Mark?'

'I don't know.'

'*Exactly*. It could've been anyone, they just happened to pick on you. Because everyone has something they'd like to go back and change.'

'I just want to save one person,' sniffed Mark, wiping more tears from his eyes. 'Do you have any idea what it's been like, these last nine years? All the good people who have died, where I've stood by and done nothing. How do you think I felt on September the 11th, watching all those people die? But I did *nothing*. I could've saved my own father, but I did *nothing*. I followed the rules, Doctor. I did as I was told. I just want one life. Is that too much to ask?'

'Yes,' said the Doctor regretfully. 'I'm afraid it is. You can't change the past.'

'Can't he?' said Amy. She had tears streaming down her cheeks. 'You're always saying time can be rewritten. Why not now?'

'Because this isn't about one person's life,' explained the Doctor. 'The Angels have arranged this deliberately so that any change in the timeline will have the greatest possible impact.'

'But there's got to be some way of saving her,' cried Amy. 'There has to be something we can do!'

'No. Rebecca's death is a complex space-time event. If Mark prevents it, he won't just change the future, he'll change the past as well.'

The poor guy, thought Rory. All he wants to do is to save his wife's life. Rory thought about what he would do if he was in Mark's shoes, and it was Amy who was about to die. Would he risk everything just for the slightest possibility of saving her? Of course he would. Like a shot. Because the thought of her death, the thought of having to go on living without her, was simply too terrible to imagine.

Rory wiped the tears from his eyes and swung his torch around him again, almost grateful for the distraction. While the two Angels on either side of Mark hadn't moved, the others had each taken three or four steps closer and had raised their arms to either side. Closing off any gaps between them.

'You're lying!' cried Mark. 'You can't know any of this for sure!'

'Mark, if you save her, what do you think will happen?' said the Doctor. 'You think you'll just get to carry on from where you left off?'

'No—'

'No. You'll wipe out the events of the next eight years. All that time will be unwritten. But that's not all you'll lose. You'll lose the *past* nine years too. All the time you had with Rebecca will cease to have existed. All gone. Not even a memory. Every moment you ever spent with her will be lost without trace!'

'Why?'

'Think. You've *travelled in time*. Your past, present and future are inextricably bound up together. Think of all the times you've intervened in your own past. Would you have even got together with Rebecca in the first place if it hadn't been for your future self? No. But if she never died, you'd never have travelled back and so you'd never have got together. That whole timeline will be erased.'

'I don't believe you,' stammered Mark. 'I don't believe you!'

'You'll lose her, Mark. And the Angels will feed, and they will grow stronger. And that will be the beginning of the end of the Earth.'

'What? How do you know that?'

'Because I've seen it *before*! Do you think when the Angels are done with you that'll be the end of it? No. They'll move onto someone else. Put them through everything you've been through until they create another paradox. Then there'll be someone else, and someone else, until there isn't a single person left on this planet whose life hasn't been used by the Angels as a source of nutrition.' The Doctor raised his eyebrows and spoke softly, pleadingly. 'And I won't be able to stop them. They're weak now but they won't remain weak for long. You're just the first. But you won't be the last.'

Mark's face crumpled in pain. 'I just want to save her.'

'I'm sorry,' said the Doctor, with the sadness of centuries. 'But you've got to let her go.'

Fez Rory coughed to get the Doctor's attention. While the Doctor had been trying to make Mark see sense, the four Weeping Angels had advanced even closer. They were now standing only four or five metres away, each with their arms outstretched, their faces eerily calm. 'Er, Doctor, hate to interrupt, but we have a Weeping Angel situation here.'

'It's like they're waiting for something,' said Amy from somewhere behind Rory. 'Why haven't they attacked?'

'They're running low on fuel,' said the Doctor. 'They won't do anything unless we try to escape or get to Mark's car. They'll want to conserve their energy until the paradox takes place.'

'And then?' said Rory nervously.

'Oh, then we're all dead,' said the Doctor nonchalantly. 'It's either us or Rebecca.' He turned back to Mark. The two Weeping Angels were now between him and the Doctor. Mark stood staring at them in horror, stumbling backwards. Then he turned and broke into a run, quickly disappearing into the total darkness.

'So what do you suggest we do now?' said Rory, waving his torch between the Angels. They were getting closer all the time. Soon they'd be within touching distance.

'Rory. You know how you've always wanted to be my secretary?'

'No.'

'Well now's your chance.' The Doctor rummaged in his pockets and retrieved a notepad and pencil. He rapidly scribbled a note on the pad, before handing it to Rory along with the wallet containing his psychic paper. 'Look after this for me. May come in handy.' He flipped a card out of his sleeve like a magician and gave it to Rory. 'Psychic credit card, don't go mad.'

'Sorry, why are you giving me your stuff?' said Rory, putting the pad, wallet and card in his jacket. 'And what do you mean, "come in handy"?'

'You're going to run a little errand for me.' The Doctor raised his eyebrows at Fez Rory as though checking something. Fez Rory nodded. The Doctor nodded back, then turned to Rory and gave him a reassuring smile which only served to make him more worried. 'I need you to pop back to the TARDIS. You think you can do that?'

Rory aimed his torch at the nearest Weeping Angel,

the one cutting off their route back up the hill. It reached out towards him with both arms. If he was quick, he might be able to slip past it. 'I'll give it my best shot,' said Rory. 'But you still haven't —'

'Then go,' urged the Doctor. 'Now! *Go!*'

Rory took a deep breath and hurled himself towards the Weeping Angel. All the time concentrating on keeping his torch trained on its face and not blinking.

Without warning his right foot snagged on what felt like a length of rope and Rory tripped over, landing heavily on his front. The torch rolled out of his fingers. For a moment, Rory had the sensation of being extremely cold and damp, his hands and face drenched in slimy mud. He strained his eyes to look around him but could only see darkness. He reached out, desperately trying to find the torch. But instead he felt the touch of something made of stone.

And then Rory wasn't in 2003 any more.

Chapter 17

'Rory!' screamed Amy. 'Rory! No!'

It had happened in an instant. There hadn't been a flash or a sound. Rory had simply disappeared into the blackness like a light being switched off. Amy aimed her torch towards where she'd heard him fall. The thin light picked out an empty patch of glistening grass and a Weeping Angel, reaching down towards the ground with an outstretched hand.

Amy's heart pounded. He'd gone. Her brave husband Rory had gone. He'd been touched by a Weeping Angel.

'It's all right,' said future Rory, removing his Fez. 'He's just been sent back to 2001. Didn't hurt a bit. Though you do get this sort of garlic-y taste in your mouth which takes ages to shift.'

'You mean, that was how you ended up back there...' Amy turned and thumped the Doctor on the arm. 'You *knew* that would happen!'

The Doctor nodded, then looked up in alarm.

There was another flash of blue lightning and a clap of thunder. But instead of fading, the lightning lingered, sending bright trails of light zigzagging across the grass like bouncing snakes.

'Rory,' said the Doctor. 'Did you manage to complete my little errand?'

'Little errand?' said Rory. 'Hardly *little*. Insanely complicated, more like!'

'Sorry, what errand would that be?' said Amy.

'Just before Rory went back in time I jotted down a note,' said the Doctor, his eyes darting between the six Angels that surrounded them, as though daring them to move. 'Containing instructions on what to do when he arrived in 2001. Well?'

'Yeah, I did it,' Rory sighed. 'Took me four weeks to convince the farmer I wasn't having a laugh. If I got it right, the "on" switch should be on the ground somewhere around here.'

'What "on" switch?' said Amy as the Doctor and Rory swept their torch lights over the turf at their feet.

'Here it is! Yes! You beauty!' announced Rory. The beam of his torch illuminated a thick cable twisting through the grass. It was so well-concealed, Amy would never have spotted it if she hadn't been looking for it. With a start she realised that it was this cable that Rory – the other Rory, the one who had vanished – had tripped over only a few seconds ago.

'What's that doing there?' said Amy. 'Will somebody *please* tell me what's going on!'

Rory's beam ran along the cable to where it joined several other cables at a black box with a big red switch. All very heavy-duty, the sort of thing you'd expect to find backstage at a rock concert.

'Found it!' announced Rory joyfully, before he gave a frightened yelp as his torchlight illuminated the two motionless white figures that were standing on either side of the switch, their hands outstretched, leering at him mockingly. 'Oh. Whoops.'

The Weeping Angels were between them and the black box. Whatever that red switch did, there was no way they could reach it.

His heart thumping hard in his chest, Mark paused to catch his breath as he reached the gate, drawing in deep lungfuls of ice-cold air, lifting his head to let the rain cool his face.

His SUV remained in the road, its lights on full-beam. Mark glanced up and down the lane, but found no sign of any traffic. But in a couple of minutes, a heavy goods lorry would be accelerating down that lane towards him.

Mark wiped his eyes, wet with rain and aching from tears, and glanced back up into the field. Electric torches danced in the darkness. The Doctor, Amy, Rory and the other Rory in a Fez. Except there seemed to be only the three of them now. The Angels had formed a ring around them, as though performing a circle dance.

There was another rumble of thunder and flicker of electric blue light.

The Doctor's words echoed in his ears. 'It's either us or Rebecca.' And what had he done? He'd run away and left them to die. But that wasn't his fault, Mark told himself. He couldn't save them, not from the Weeping

Angels. He couldn't.

That wasn't the only thing the Doctor had said that preyed on his mind. If he saved Rebecca, then according to the Doctor he would change not just the future, but the past. He would lose not just all those long, lonely years of grief, but also all the time he'd had with her.

Because if he'd never travelled in time, everything would have been different. That night at the students' union when they'd kissed on the rooftop wouldn't have happened. He probably wouldn't have gone to Rome with her, he wouldn't have been able to afford it if his future self hadn't given him that winning lottery ticket. And even if he had gone, he wouldn't have got his wallet back after it was stolen so they wouldn't have gone to the Capitoline Museum. And they wouldn't have got together at the museum had it not been for his future self, the Doctor, Amy and Rory locking them in.

Mark thought back to all the other times he'd had with Rebecca. The most precious pages in his book of memories. All the times he'd met her for coffee to discuss their relationship troubles. The day they moved into their first flat together. Their wedding day. And the time after Rebecca had been in that accident and they'd spent two weeks in their flat together, watching videos and DVDs.

The saddest part of all was that there weren't enough memories. He wanted more. He deserved more. He regretted to the core of his being all the nights he'd worked late when he could have been with Rebecca.

He would give anything, anything in the world just to have one more hour with her. To have just one more memory. It had been that single driving wish, that burning feeling of injustice, that had kept him going for the past seventeen years.

He had to have Rebecca back. If he didn't, what was the point? What had it all been for?

But if what the Doctor said was true, then all those memories would be taken from him. And people would die. Innocent people would die, and it would all be because of him. Rebecca wouldn't want that. She wouldn't want to be the reason why that happened.

Mark looked back up the hill, to where the Doctor and his friends were surrounded by the Weeping Angels.

'I'm sorry,' choked Mark, stifling a sob as he walked over to his car. 'I'm sorry, Rebecca.'

Rory backed away from the two Weeping Angels in front of him, flashing his torchlight from one to the other. He backed into the Doctor, busy trying to keep his own two Weeping Angels at bay. 'It's no good,' said Rory. 'I can't reach the "On" switch. I messed up, and now we're trapped and are probably going to die.'

'It's not over yet, I should be able to activate it with this,' said the Doctor, deftly raising his sonic screwdriver. Which failed to light up or make any sound. 'Oh. That would've been a lot more impressive had it actually worked. No, you were right with the first thing you said.'

There was another boom of thunder and crackle of lightning. It lit up the Angels' faces. They were snarling hungrily, their jagged teeth bared, their tongues lolling, their foreheads ridged in scowls of hatred, their eyes hideous staring blank orbs of stone.

Rory held them back using his torchlight. The light grew dimmer. Rory shook the torch and banged it with the palm of his hand, but it didn't get any brighter. 'Doctor. The torches—'

'The Angels are draining the energy,' said the Doctor. 'I know. Hence my sonic trouble.'

Rory flashed the feeble beam back towards the Angels. They were now less than a metre away, reaching towards him with their long, claw-like fingers. The torchlight was now so weak he had to strain his eyes just to make out the shape of the Angels in the darkness.

'Rory,' said Amy. 'I don't think I can keep them back much—' She gave a short scream.

Rory spun around to see Amy standing perfectly still, her eyes wide with terror, a Weeping Angel's arm coiling around her neck, almost but not quite making contact with her skin. The Weeping Angel's mouth hung open lasciviously, like a vampire about to sink its fangs into her jugular.

'Don't stop looking at it, Rory', begged Amy. 'Don't look away. And please, whatever you do, d-d-don't blink!'

Rory kept his eyes glued to the Weeping Angel, but as the light from his torch faded away, it slowly but surely disappeared into the darkness.

Suddenly the roar of a car engine filled the air and Amy and the Weeping Angel were caught in the lurching beams of an approaching pair of headlights. Rory didn't dare look away from Amy, he didn't dare blink, even as he heard the car draw nearer and come to a halt, even as he heard the sound of the car door slamming and someone running towards them.

'Mark,' shouted the Doctor. 'Press the big red switch! On the ground by your feet!'

K-chunk! K-chunk! K-chunk!

There was a brilliant, dazzling light. Temporarily blinded, Rory blinked.

When he looked again, when his eyes adjusted to the brightness, he found that the Weeping Angel hadn't moved. It still had its arm wrapped around Amy, but the fact that the electric lamps had come on meant that the Doctor's plan had worked.

The Weeping Angels were still in a circle around them, all frozen in position as they lunged forward, clutching at the air. But outside the circle of Angels, about six metres away, there was a second circle of six powerful halogen lamps mounted at ground level, all shining inwards. And beside each of the lamps was a video camera, on a tripod, pointing inwards, and beside each camera was a television monitor showing six pictures from six different angles of the Weeping Angels. They were standing in the middle of a ring of cameras.

Mark was crouching beside the big red 'On' switch.

'It's all right,' the Doctor reassured Amy. 'They're not going to move.' With some difficulty, he helped her squeeze out of the Weeping Angel's embrace.

'What did you do?' asked Amy once she was free, shielding her eyes against the glare of the lamps.

'Nothing,' said the Doctor with a generous smile. 'You have Rory to thank for this.'

'*Rory?*' said Amy incredulously.

'Yeah, well, all in a month's work,' said Rory. 'Though to be fair, it was the Doctor's idea.' He pulled the Doctor's notebook out of his jacket. Flipping open the cover, he showed Amy the contents; a page of almost illegible instructions from the Doctor on what to do in 2001, along with a diagram on how to set up the video cameras.

'*What* was?' said Amy, turning from Angel to Angel, making sure that they'd stopped moving.

The Doctor pocketed his torch. 'It's quite simple. The Weeping Angels are quantum-locked, meaning they can only move if they're not being observed.'

'I know that, you have mentioned it once or twice.'

'So what we've done,' said the Doctor. 'Is to arrange things so that each Weeping Angel is not only being observed, but is also observing itself *and* all the other Weeping Angels.'

Amy peered at one of the monitors. 'You mean this is showing the pictures from all the cameras at once?'

'And there's nowhere you can stand where you're not looking towards one of the monitors,' said Rory. 'Every direction is covered.' It had taken him the best part of a month to set it all up; travelling down to locate the exact spot, then persuading a video equipment company to not only set up a specific arrangement of lights, cameras and monitors, but to do it on a specific date, two years in the future. And then he'd had to convince the farmer who owned the land to let them do this. Rory had only managed to get everything sorted the evening before he was due to meet the Doctor and Amy. If he'd learned one thing during his time in 2001, it was this; it's amazing what people will agree to if you're prepared to pay cash in advance.

When they'd first arrived in the TARDIS, he'd been terrified that the Doctor might lead them to the wrong part of the field. But he needn't have worried; of course they would all end up in the right spot, because that's what they'd done last time. And although Rory had caught the occasional glimpse of the cameras, lamps and monitors, because he knew where to look, they were all sufficiently well hidden by the grass not to be seen by the Doctor, Amy, his former self – or, more importantly, by the Angels.

'So you led the Angels into a trap?' said Amy. 'Using us as the bait!'

'Bait and switch! They should know better than to put me in a trap!' The Doctor walked over to Mark. 'You came back,' said the Doctor delicately.

Mark nodded, blinking back tears, his breathing shallow. 'I could hardly let you die, could I?'

'Had me worried for a moment there, though,' said the Doctor.

'Doctor! The Angels!' shouted Amy.

Rory turned to see the five Weeping Angels begin to flicker and fade away, like the picture on a television screen during interference.

'They're too weak to maintain their corporeal forms,' explained the Doctor. 'And as they're quantum-locked, there's only one way left for them to go…'

In a few moments they were all transparent, their stonework fizzling like static, and then, in an instant, they all vanished.

'Go?' said Amy. 'Go where?'

The Doctor nodded to one of the monitors. On the screen Rory could see the Weeping Angel, staring out at him in grainy, flickering black-and-white, its hands pressed against the glass as though it was trying to break through. Rory looked in the next monitor along. The story was the same. Each screen showed an Angel, trapped behind the glass, an indistinct grey mass.

'*Caught in a closed circuit!* This is our chance. Do what I do!' The Doctor rushed over to one of the cameras, lifted it by the tripod, then positioned it so that it faced towards the monitor to which it was connected.

'What *are* you doing?' asked Rory.

The Doctor flicked a switch. 'I'm sending them into infinity.'

The Weeping Angel on the screen gained a line of identical, ghostly Angels behind it. This then dissolved into a swirling, looping pattern of fog which rapidly faded to blackness.

The Doctor, Amy and Rory repeated the process on the remaining Angels. It was only when they reached the sixth monitor and discovered that it was blank that Rory realised something was amiss. 'Doctor. One of our Weeping Angels is missing.'

'What?'

'There were six. One of them must've got away.'

The Doctor looked briefly alarmed, but then he peered up at the night sky. There hadn't been a rumble of thunder or flash of lightning since Mark had returned. The Doctor turned towards him. 'You moved your car,' said the Doctor. 'There's not going to be a paradox. History isn't going to be changed. That's what weakened the Angels...'

Mark nodded sadly and then turned back down the hill. The headlights of a heavy goods lorry flashed out of the darkness. It accelerated down the steep country lane, past where Mark's car had been parked, and onwards into the night.

And then, just for a moment, the lorry's red tail-lights illuminated the shape of a figure at the edge of the field. 'Doctor, the Weeping Angel!' said Rory 'Where's it going?'

'The scene of the accident,' said the Doctor bleakly. He began to stride down the hill towards where the Angel had been standing. 'Come on.'

They didn't see the crash. But they could see the orange warning lights that blinked on and off, lighting up the hedges that loomed over the lane.

The lorry had come to a rest halfway up the hedge, the cabin tilted onto its side, its radiator grille steaming, its warning lights flashing. The driver was slumped unconscious on his steering wheel.

'You leave the driver to us.' The Doctor patted Mark's back. 'Be with her.'

Mark looked around in a daze, unable to take it all in, and then he spotted Rebecca's car. The force of the collision had sent it into the next field, rolling over until it came to a rest upside down. Thick smoke poured out of the engine and he could see the tell-tale flicker of flames.

Standing about six metres from the car, caught in the sickly orange glow of the warning light, was the remaining Weeping Angel.

*

Looking out across the field, Rebecca wondered why everything had an odd orange hue, as though lit by a street lamp. Her seatbelt was so tight she could hardly breathe. She wanted to wipe the rain from her eyes, but her hands didn't respond.

Now that was weird. About six metres away, in the field, stood a statue, like might be found in a graveyard, or a Roman museum. It was a statue of a young woman with coiled hair, a flowing robe and two wings. An angel. The statue was hunched, burying its head in its hands.

The orange light blinked off, and Rebecca thought of childhood bonfires.

The orange light blinked on again. The statue of the angel was now staring towards her with blank, pupil-less eyes.

The light blinked off and on again, and each time the statue drew closer, closer, until it filled her view, looming over her, reaching out towards her with hands like talons.

Rebecca wished that Mark was here.

And he was. The statue had vanished and Mark had taken its place. He leaned into the car and gently brushed the rain from her face. He smiled at her tenderly. She could see tears streaming down his face.

Why did he look so old? His hair was thin and flecked with grey, his skin was weathered and his eyes were lined with crow's feet. They were the sad, tired eyes of a man who had suffered years of sleepless nights. But they were still the same eyes she'd fallen in love with, and they were still full of love for her.

Rebecca attempted to say his name, but no words

came. She wanted to ask him what he was doing here. He should be working at the office in Croydon, not out here in the depths of Sussex in the wind and rain with her.

She felt him take her hand and squeeze it. His skin felt so warm against hers, like fire. Looking up at him, into his sad, tired eyes, she smiled. Because Mark was here. She knew everything would be all right.

And then Rebecca Whitaker felt no more worries, no more fears, no more pain. She slipped away into death with her head cradled in her husband's arms.

Amy, the Doctor and Rory watched in a respectful silence as Mark released Rebecca from her car and placed her body on the grass a short distance away.

Amy sniffed and wiped the tears from her eyes. 'He couldn't save her.'

'He never could,' said the Doctor. 'The Angels just made him believe that, to serve their own ends.'

'So time can't be rewritten?'

'Not without people getting hurt,' said the Doctor ruefully.

'What about the Weeping Angel?' asked Rory. 'Where did that go?'

'It escaped.' The Doctor indicated a metal box perched in the hedge by the side of the road a few metres from where the lorry had come to rest. The speed camera reflected the glow of the lorry's warning lights as they blinked on and off.

'But if it's in the speed cameras, it could go anywhere…' said Rory. 'We have to find it.'

'There's no need,' said the Doctor. 'That's the

Weeping Angel we encountered when we first arrived, in 2011. The Angel trapped inside a television.'

'You mean, the one that sent Mark back to 2003?' said Amy.

The Doctor nodded. 'In a desperate attempt to break the time loop. But by trying to change history, it ends up creating it. A prisoner of its own past.'

'But why wait until 2011?'

'Recharging its batteries? And it couldn't send Mark back until he'd received the letter. The letter I imagine they dropped off at Mark's office a couple of days ago.'

Another minute passed in silence, then Mark returned. His eyes were raw from tears and his breathing was shallow and weak, as though each inhalation caused him pain.

In the distance Amy could see the headlights of a car through the trees. The driver that would be the first on the scene, the one who would call the emergency services.

'Come on,' said the Doctor. 'Time we were gone.'

Mark was about to leave the office at Pollard & Boyce when his mobile rang. He checked the clock. Who would be ringing him at five past eleven at night? He pulled his phone out of his pocket. The caller ID read *Rodney Coles*.

Mark pressed answer. 'Hello, yes?'

'Mark, it's, um, Rodney. Rebecca's father.' He sounded oddly frail and distant, pausing between his words.

'Rodney. What is it?'

'It…' There was a long silence. 'There's been an accident, Mark. Rebecca has been in an accident. She was driving home to see us when…' There was another long silence, leaving Mark listening to nothing but a faint hiss.

Mark swallowed and walked unsteadily over to his desk. He felt like he was standing at the top of a very high cliff, looking down over the edge. 'She's all right, though, isn't she? Tell me she's all right.'

'I'm sorry, Mark,' said Rodney. 'She's gone. She, um, when they found her, she'd already, they said, she'd already died.'

Rebecca was dead. Mark couldn't believe it. Even saying the words in his head, he couldn't believe it. He felt like he was suffocating. His lips were dry, his heart felt as heavy as a stone and there was a terrible twisting sensation in his stomach. He felt like everything around him was suddenly distant, unreal, like he was watching someone else in a movie. Or a bad dream from which he might wake up at any moment.

But he wasn't going to wake up. Mark talked to Rodney for a couple of minutes but his mind was elsewhere. The call ended and he sat in silence, looking at the photograph of Rebecca he kept on his desk. The photograph of her sitting on the balcony of their hotel room in Rome, in her summer dress, gazing out into the street, the morning sun shining in her hair, a contented, secretive smile on her lips. The photograph he'd taken the morning after they'd got together.

Mark picked up the photograph, his hands trembling. Rebecca was dead. He'd lost her. He'd never hear her voice again. Mark wanted to scream.

He wanted to fall on his knees and beg the heavens; please, take time back. Let me go back just one hour, to before Rebecca was killed so I can save her. Anything, I'll do anything, if you'll just let me go back, and for this not to be now, for this not to be real, for this not to be for ever.

Mark held the photograph to his face to try to stop himself crying, because he knew that once he'd started, he might never stop.

Epilogue

16 April 2003

Mark stood at the lychgate, the Doctor, Amy and Rory beside him, unnoticed by the mourners at the graveside. The grave had been dug on the edge of the graveyard, in the shade of an old, gnarled yew tree. The pallbearers lowered the coffin into the ground and the vicar spoke the prayer of committal, his solemn, lilting voice carrying through the warm spring air amidst the rustle of leaves and the birdsong.

It was the same vicar who'd conducted the wedding service two and a half years earlier. He was addressing the same people as at the wedding; many of the male mourners were even wearing the same suits. There was Gareth, Mr Pollard and Mr Boyce, and Rajeev, Lucy and Emma. And there were Rebecca's parents, Olivia and Rodney, both looking so tired, so stunned and lost. And there was his mother, dabbing at her eyes with a handkerchief.

And there was his younger self. Standing at his mother's side, staring into the grave, tears streaming down his cheeks. Mark could remember standing there as though it was yesterday. He could still feel the grief, like a huge weight pressing down on his chest. But as he remembered it, the day of the funeral had been a cold, grim overcast day. He hadn't remembered it taking place on a sunny day under a clear blue sky.

The service ended, and Mark turned to the Doctor, Amy and Rory, who had stood beside him throughout. Their eyes glistened with tears. It must be strange for them, Mark thought. As far as the Doctor and Amy were concerned, they had only met a few days ago. It must be strange and heartbreaking to travel in time as they do. But maybe not as strange and heartbreaking as it had been for him.

'Enough,' said Mark. 'Enough. Can I go back now?'

'Not just yet. There's one more thing you have to see.'

8 May 1993

The guitar riff of 'Two Princes' echoed out of the open doors of the Dunmore hall of residence and into the cool spring evening. Students stretched out on the freshly cut grass with folders of notes and paperback books. Everyone looked so young, so carefree.

Beaming at everyone he passed as though they were old friends, the Doctor led Mark, Rory and Amy into the student hall. For Mark, it was an unnerving experience. He'd spent his first year at university living in this building. It was both strange and familiar, as he saw so many details he'd long since forgotten. The posters on the noticeboard gave details of NUS demonstrations, of upcoming gigs, and of the opening hours of the computer centre.

A hall party was in progress. From one end of the corridor could be heard the glam jangle of the new Suede album. They squeezed past the students lining the hall and entered the communal kitchen. There, the Doctor indicated for Mark to look across the room.

To see Rebecca, leaning against the far wall, paper cup in hand, a sardonic smile on her lips. Her long hair had been dyed black and she wore an American college sweatshirt.

'Speak to her,' said the Doctor, adjusting his bow tie with a cheerful waggle.

'Are you sure? Won't I be changing history?'

'I'm not expecting you to give her a list of future presidents of the United States.' The Doctor nudged Mark forward. 'Speak to her.'

Mark took a deep breath and walked towards her, feeling as self-conscious as he had when he was a 19-year-old student. Even though he was now 46 years old.

'Hi,' he said to Rebecca. 'Do you mind if I have a quick word?'

'No, no, not at all.' She sized him up and frowned. 'Mature student, right?'

'Yeah. Something like that.'

'Interesting,' Rebecca smiled. 'So what was it you wanted to talk to me about?'

Mark told her everything. He was careful to leave

out the dates, names, and time travel, but he told her all about the beautiful girl he'd met and fallen in love with twenty-seven years earlier, who, after several false starts and wrong turnings, he'd made his wife. He told her how happy they'd been together. And he told her how his wife had been killed in a traffic accident, and how, ever since, a single hour hadn't passed without him thinking about her.

Rebecca listened with intense concentration. 'She sounds great, this – what was her name?'

'Um, Rebecca, actually.'

'Spooky, that's my name.' Rebecca grimaced at the contents of her cup. 'Though no one calls me that and lives. So how long ago has it been since she died, if you don't mind me asking?'

'Seventeen years.'

'Seventeen *years*?' repeated Rebecca in astonishment. 'Whoa. Long time.'

'Not that long.'

Rebecca paused to consider her next words carefully. 'Tell me to shut up if I'm speaking out of turn, but, well, everything you've said so far has been about you, about how *you* feel. Haven't you ever stopped to consider what Rebecca would want in all this?'

'What *Rebecca* would want?'

'Would she want you to be miserable for the rest of your life? Would she want you to spend all your time on your own, wishing for what might have been? No.'

'No?'

'No. She'd want you to be happy. She'd want you to find somebody else, somebody else who makes you happy. That's what I'd want, if I was her.'

'I'm not sure I can.'

'You don't know until you've tried. That's an *order*.' Rebecca smiled at him irreverently, her eyes twinkling as she looked up at him and stroked him gently on the cheek. 'Do that for me.'

Mark stared at her for a second, struck dumb. His cheek tingled. Then he turned back towards the door, where the Doctor, Amy and Rory were waiting. 'Thanks,' said Mark. 'I will.'

'Glad to be of service.'

Mark returned to the Doctor and his friends, who looked at him questioningly. Had he got the answer he wanted? Mark nodded.

'You'll always have the time you had with Rebecca,' the Doctor told him. 'No one can take that away from you.'

'I know,' said Mark. 'I know that now.'

'Then I think it's time to say goodbye.'

Bex watched the man leave the kitchen. He seemed like such a lovely guy, so sweet and so sad. It had been strange, speaking to him; it was like they'd known each other for years. She hoped he'd follow her advice and find someone.

Her thoughts were interrupted by a cry of indignation from the hallway. A young man she'd never seen before stumbled into the kitchen, his neck and T-shirt soaked with red wine. He looked so ridiculous, Bex couldn't help but laugh. 'Would you believe it?' he muttered in response to her amusement. 'Some stupid bloke in a tweed jacket just banged into me, making me spill red wine all over myself.'

'Yeah,' said Bex sympathetically. 'I can see that.'

'My best shirt, this is, you know. Ruined.'

'No, you should be able to get it out if you pour hot water through it straight away.' Bex indicated the kitchen sink with her cup. 'But you have to do it straight away.'

The young man sighed and pulled his T-shirt over his head. Giving Bex the chance to admire his bare chest. For a skinny little thing, he was surprisingly well-defined.

He put his T-shirt in the sink and ran it under the hot tap. While he tried in vain to remove the wine, Bex studied him. He had short brown hair, gelled into a parting, and wore John Lennon-style glasses. He was quite cute. And there was something strangely familiar about him.

'Hey, have I just met your dad?' said Bex.

'What?'

'I was just speaking to bloke who looks just like you, but older.'

'Really?' said the young man. 'You'll have to point him out to me.' He inspected his T-shirt. 'Well, I think I've got most of it out. Thanks.' He turned towards her. 'I'm Mark, by the way. Mark Whitaker.'

'Bex Coles.'

'Cool name.' Mark looked at her, as though he was about to speak, but no words came. Bex tried not to laugh out loud at his awkwardness. 'Um, yeah, er. I don't suppose you fancy, you know, going out some time?'

'What sort of thing did you have in mind?'

'Well, there's this band on at the Whip-Round next

week who I've heard great things about. Apparently they're going to be bigger than Suede or Blur.'

'Really? What are they called?'

'Echobelly.'

'I shall have to make a note of that, then,' said Bex. 'So you don't have a girlfriend then?'

Mark paused before answering. 'No. You?'

'No, and I don't have a boyfriend either.'

'So? Do you fancy going to this thing with me?'

'Yeah, why not?'

Bex heard someone coming in and turned to see her boyfriend Dennis McCormack standing in the doorway, dressed, as usual, in a ridiculously formal jacket that showed off just how overweight he was. 'Hi, babes. Surprise, yeah?' He glanced at Mark standing at the sink with his shirt off. This puzzled Dennis. 'Why haven't you got a shirt on?'

'Red wine,' explained Mark.

'Ah, right,' said Dennis, returning his attention to Bex. 'Anyway, turns out the debating society dinner was dead, so I thought, Dennis, doesn't do to keep the lady waiting.' With that, he kissed her on the lips and attacked her mouth like it was a lick-before-sealing envelope.

When Dennis finally allowed her to come up for air, Bex noticed that they'd been joined by a girl with an unwieldy chest and a severely cut bob of auburn hair. 'Hey, Mark,' said the girl, giving him a peck on the cheek. 'Who are you talking to?'

'Um. This is Bex,' said Mark. 'And—'

'McCormack, Dennis,' said Dennis, grabbing Mark's hand and pumping it vigorously.

'Aren't you going to introduce me, Mark?' prompted the girl.

'Oh. Yes. This is Sophie, my, um, girlfriend,' said Mark.

'Nice to meet you,' said Bex.

'Why haven't you got your shirt on?' Sophie asked Mark.

'Red wine,' explained Dennis.

'Well we can't have you standing around half-naked, can we?' said Sophie, taking Mark by the hand. 'Come on, I'll find you another shirt.' She led him out of the kitchen. Bex watched them go, thinking what a pity it was that Mark had a girlfriend and she had a boyfriend. If they'd both been single, this could've been the beginning of something.

Mark's cheek was still tingling when he stepped back inside the TARDIS. The Doctor danced around the console, flicking switches and, after a few moments, the central column began to rise and fall.

The tingling sensation spread from Mark's cheek across his face and down his neck. It prickled like pins and needles. 'Doctor...' he said.

The Doctor glanced towards him and recoiled in shock. 'Oh my,' he breathed, staring at Mark as though there was something wrong with his face.

'What is it?' asked Mark, touching his cheek. His skin felt odd. Softer, smoother. He turned to Amy and Rory, who were both gawping at him in amazement. 'What's happening?'

'Amy,' said the Doctor. 'Mirror!'

Amy fished a small hand mirror out from her coat

and handed it to Mark. He lifted it to study his reflection. The face that stared back wasn't that of a man in his late forties. It was the face of a much younger man, a man growing younger all the time. As he watched, the lines around his eyes faded away, his hair grew thicker and all the grey hairs turned brown.

The tingling continued down his arms to the ends of his fingers. Mark watched as the wrinkles on his hands smoothed away. The sensation spread down to his toes, then faded.

'When Rebecca touched your face, she shorted out the time differential,' explained the Doctor matter-of-factly. 'She's given you the past nine years of your life back. You're the same age now as you were when we first met you. It'll be as if you'd never spent all those years in the past.'

'But I can still remember them.'

'Oh, they still *happened* all right,' grinned the Doctor. 'It's just that you're not a day older, that's all.'

Mark returned the mirror to Amy, barely able to believe the truth. He was young again. Well, 37 years old. And all it had taken was one touch from Rebecca's hand.

14 October 2011

It was a cold, drizzly evening, just like the evening when he'd first met the Doctor, Amy and Rory. The streets were dotted with puddles and thunder rumbled in the distance. They'd materialised a few minutes' walk from his flat, and just as they were turning into the street, the Doctor ordered them to stay back and keep out of sight. Peering out from behind a recycling bin, Mark soon discovered the reason why.

On the pavement stood a blue police box, and standing at the entrance of the block of flats he could see *another* Doctor, Amy and Rory. He watched as they hurried into the TARDIS. Seconds later, it faded from view with a groaning, wrenching sound.

'OK, they're gone,' said the Doctor, straightening up and wringing his hands. They walked the remaining few metres to the path leading up to entrance, then the Doctor halted. 'Well, this is where we came in, more or less. One week after you were touched by the Weeping Angel.'

'One week?' Mark patted his pockets. 'Oh. Hang on a minute…'

Rory smiled and passed him his house keys. 'Been looking after them for you. Say hi to Mrs Levenson from me, I've been, um, flat-sitting for the last week.'

'Right,' said Mark.

'Oh, and you're out of milk,' added Rory. 'And tea. And bread. And toilet paper.'

'Thanks,' said Mark, turning to Amy. 'Thanks for everything.'

'It was a pleasure,' said Amy with an affectionate smirk.

'Goodbye,' said the Doctor. 'And good luck in the, ah, future. Where, fortunately, the rules of time mean that you can do *whatever* you want.' He beamed, patted Mark on the shoulder, and turned to go. Rory shook Mark's hand, Amy kissed him on the cheek, and then the three of them walked away, back down the street to the TARDIS.

Mark walked up the stairs to the entrance. He paused before slipping the key in the lock. Just as he had done before a week ago, nine years ago.

He was back in 2011, but now things would be different. He still owned Harold Jones's property, stocks and shares. He was still a multi-millionaire. He didn't have to go back to work at Pollard, Boyce & Whitaker, not if he didn't want to. He could do anything he wanted.

The first thing he would do, he decided, would be to go and see Lucy and Emma. He hadn't seen them for years but he knew they wouldn't mind if he turned up out of the blue and spent an evening talking to them about Rebecca. Not because he wanted to talk about her death or how much he missed her, but because he wanted to remember her and celebrate her life with friends, because the memory of her no longer made him feel sad.

He'd take her advice, Mark decided, and find somebody. But where to look? He didn't have the faintest idea. But it would be fun finding out.

Mark unlocked the door and entered the block of flats, ready to begin the rest of his life.

Acknowledgements

Thanks to Justin Richards for giving me the chance to show off; to Steven Moffat for letting me borrow his best monsters; and to the following, who made this book better: Stephen Aintree, Steve Berry, Debbie Challis, Robert Dick, Debbie Hill, Matt Kimpton, Joe Lidster and Simon Guerrier.

Available now from BBC Books:

DOCTOR WHO

Apollo 23

by Justin Richards

£6.99 ISBN 978 1 846 07200 0

An astronaut in full spacesuit appears out of thin air in a busy shopping centre. Maybe it's a publicity stunt.

A photo shows a well-dressed woman in a red coat lying dead at the edge of a crater on the dark side of the moon, beside her beloved dog 'Poochie'. Maybe it's a hoax.

But as the Doctor and Amy find out, these are just minor events in a sinister plan to take over every human being on Earth. The plot centres on a secret military base on the moon – that's where Amy and the TARDIS are.

The Doctor is back on Earth, and without the TARDIS there's no way he can get to the moon to save Amy and defeat the aliens.

Or is there? The Doctor discovers one last great secret that could save humanity: Apollo 23.

A thrilling, all-new adventure featuring the Doctor and Amy, as played by Matt Smith and Karen Gillan in the spectacular hit series from BBC Television.

Available now from BBC Books:

by David Llewellyn

£6.99 ISBN 978 1 846 07969 6

250,000 years' worth of junk floating in deep space, home to the shipwrecked Sittuun, the carnivorous Sollogs, and worst of all – the Humans.

The Doctor and Amy arrive on this terrifying world in the middle of an all-out frontier war between Sittuun and Humans, and the clock is already ticking. There's a comet in the sky, and it's on a collision course with the Gyre...

When the Doctor is kidnapped, it's up to Amy and 'galaxy-famous swashbuckler' Dirk Slipstream to save the day.

But who is Slipstream, exactly? And what is he really doing here?

A thrilling, all-new adventure featuring the Doctor and Amy, as played by Matt Smith and Karen Gillan in the spectacular hit series from BBC Television.

Available now from BBC Books:

DOCTOR WHO
The Forgotten Army

by Brian Minchin

£6.99 ISBN 978 1 846 07987 0

New York – one of the greatest cities on 21st-century Earth... But what's going on in the Museum? And is that really a Woolly Mammoth rampaging down Broadway?

An ordinary day becomes a time of terror, as Ice Age creatures come back to life, and the Doctor and Amy meet a new and deadly enemy. The vicious Army of the Vykoid are armed to the teeth and determined to enslave the human race. Even though they're only three inches high.

With the Vykoid army swarming across Manhattan and sealing it from the world with a powerful alien forcefield, Amy has just 24 hours to find the Doctor and save the city. If she doesn't, the people of Manhattan will be taken to work in the doomed asteroid mines of the Vykoid home planet.

But as time starts to run out, who can she trust? And how far will she have to go to free New York from the Forgotten Army?

A thrilling, all-new adventure featuring the Doctor and Amy, as played by Matt Smith and Karen Gillan in the spectacular hit series from BBC Television.

Available now from BBC Books:

DOCTOR WHO

The TARDIS Handbook

by Steve Tribe

£12.99 ISBN 978 1 846 07986 3

The inside scoop on 900 years of travel aboard the Doctor's famous time machine.

Everything you need to know about the TARDIS is here – where it came from, where it's been, how it works, and how it has changed since we first encountered it in that East London junkyard in 1963.

Including photographs, design drawings and concept artwork from different eras of the series, this handbook explores the ship's endless interior, looking inside its wardrobe and bedrooms, its power rooms and sick bay, its corridors and cloisters, and revealing just how the show's production teams have created the dimensionally transcendental police box, inside and out.

The TARDIS Handbook is the essential guide to the best ship in the universe.

Available now from BBC Books:

DOCTOR WHO
Nuclear Time

by Oli Smith

£6.99 ISBN 978 1 846 07989 4

Colorado, 1981. The Doctor, Amy and Rory arrive in Appletown – an idyllic village in the remote American desert where the townsfolk go peacefully about their suburban routines. But when two more strangers arrive, things begin to change.

The first is a mad scientist – whose warnings are cut short by an untimely and brutal death. The second is the Doctor…

As death falls from the sky, the Doctor is trapped. The TARDIS is damaged, and the Doctor finds he is living backwards through time. With Amy and Rory being hunted through the suburban streets of the Doctor's own future and getting farther away with every passing second, he must unravel the secrets of Appletown before time runs out…

A thrilling, all-new adventure featuring the Doctor, Amy and Rory, as played by Matt Smith, Karen Gillan and Arthur Darvill in the spectacular hit series from BBC Television.

Available now from BBC Books:

DOCTOR WHO
The King's Dragon

by Una McCormack

£6.99 ISBN 978 1 846 07990 0

In the city-state of Geath, the King lives in a golden hall, and the people want for nothing. Everyone is happy and everyone is rich. Or so it seems.

When the Doctor, Amy and Rory look beneath the surface, they discover a city of secrets. In dark corners, strange creatures are stirring. At the heart of the hall, a great metal dragon oozes gold. Then the Herald appears, demanding the return of her treasure... And next come the gunships.

The battle for possession of the treasure has begun, and only the Doctor and his friends can save the people of the city from being destroyed in the crossfire of an ancient civil war. But will the King surrender his new-found wealth? Or will he fight to keep it...?

A thrilling, all-new adventure featuring the Doctor, Amy and Rory, as played by Matt Smith, Karen Gillan and Arthur Darvill in the spectacular hit series from BBC Television.

Available now from BBC Books:

DOCTOR WHO
The Glamour Chase

by Gary Russell

£6.99 ISBN 978 1 846 07988 7

An archaeological dig in 1936 unearths relics of another time… And – as the Doctor, Amy and Rory realise – another place. Another planet.

But if Enola Porter, noted adventuress, has really found evidence of an alien civilisation, how come she isn't famous? Why has Rory never heard of her? Added to that, since Amy's been travelling with him for a while now, why does she now think the Doctor is from Mars?

As the ancient spaceship reactivates, the Doctor discovers that nothing and no one can be trusted. The things that seem most real could actually be literal fabrications – and very deadly indeed.

Who can the Doctor believe when no one is what they seem? And how can he defeat an enemy who can bend matter itself to their will? For the Doctor, Amy and Rory – and all of humanity – the buried secrets of the past are very much a threat to the present...

A thrilling, all-new adventure featuring the Doctor, Amy and Rory, as played by Matt Smith, Karen Gillan and Arthur Darvill in the spectacular hit series from BBC Television.

Available now from BBC Books:

DOCTOR WHO
The Only Good Dalek

by Justin Richards and Mike Collins

£16.99 ISBN 978 1 846 07984 9

Station 7 is where the Earth Forces send all the equipment captured in their unceasing war against the Daleks. It's where Dalek technology is analysed and examined. It's where the Doctor and Amy have just arrived. But somehow the Daleks have found out about Station 7 – and there's something there that they want back.

With the Doctor increasingly worried about the direction the Station's research is taking, the commander of Station 7 knows he has only one possible, desperate, defence. Because the last terrible secret of Station 7 is that they don't only store captured Dalek technology. It's also a prison. And the only thing that might stop a Dalek is another Dalek…

An epic, full-colour graphic novel featuring the Doctor and Amy, as played by Matt Smith and Karen Gillan in the spectacular hit series from BBC Television.

Available now from BBC Books:

DOCTOR WHO
The Brilliant Book 2011

Edited by Clayton Hickman

£12.99 ISBN 978 1 846 07991 7

Celebrate the rebirth of the UK's number one family drama series with this lavish hardback, containing everything you need to know about the Eleventh Doctor's first year.

Explore Amy Pond's home village, Leadworth, read a lost section from Churchill's memoirs that covers his adventures with the Doctor, and learn all about the legend of the Weeping Angels. See how the Constant Warrior protected the Pandorica over 2,000 years, how the monsters are made and discover the trade secrets of writing a thrilling *Doctor Who* script. Plus interviews with all of the key players and a few secret celebrity guests…

Including contributions from executive producer Steven Moffat, stars Matt Smith and Karen Gillan, and scriptwriters Mark Gatiss and Gareth Roberts, among others, and packed with beautiful original illustrations and never-before-seen pictures, *The Brilliant Book of Doctor Who* is the ultimate companion to the world's most successful science fiction series.

Available now from BBC Books:

DOCTOR WHO

The Coming of the Terraphiles

by Michael Moorcock

£16.99 ISBN 978 1 846 07983 2

Miggea – a star on the very edge of reality. The cusp between this universe and the next. A point where space-time has worn thin, and is in danger of collapsing… And the venue for the grand finals of the competition to win the fabled Arrow of Law.

The Doctor and Amy have joined the Terraphiles – a group dedicated to re-enacting ancient sporting events. They are determined to win the Arrow. But just getting to Miggea proves tricky. Reality is collapsing, ships are disappearing, and Captain Cornelius and his pirates are looking for easy pickings.

Even when they arrive, the Doctor and Amy's troubles won't be over. They have to find out who is so desperate to get the Arrow of Law that they will kill for it. And uncover the traitor on their own team. And win the contest fair and square.

And, of course, they need to save the universe from total destruction.

A thrilling, all-new adventure featuring the Doctor and Amy, as played by Matt Smith and Karen Gillan in the spectacular hit series from BBC Television, written by the acclaimed science fiction and fantasy author Michael Moorcock.

Available now from BBC Books:

by James Goss

£6.99 ISBN 978 1 849 90238 0

In Dr Bloom's clinic at a remote spot on the Italian coast, at the end of the eighteenth century, nothing is ever quite what it seems.

Maria is a lonely little girl with no one to play with. She writes letters to her mother from the isolated resort where she is staying. She tells of the pale English aristocrats and the mysterious Russian nobles and their attentive servants. She tells of intrigue and secrets, and she tells of strange faceless figures that rise from the sea. She writes about the enigmatic Mrs Pond who arrives with her husband and her physician, and who will change everything.

What she doesn't tell her mother is the truth that everyone knows and no one says – that the only people who come here do so to die…

A thrilling, all-new adventure featuring the Doctor, Amy and Rory, as played by Matt Smith, Karen Gillan and Arthur Darvill in the spectacular hit series from BBC Television.

Available now from BBC Books:

DOCTOR WHO

The Way through the Woods

by Una McCormack

£6.99 ISBN 978 1 849 90237 3

Two teenage girls disappear into an ancient wood, a foreboding and malevolent presence both now and in the past. The modern motorway bends to avoid it, as did the old Roman road.

In 1917 the Doctor and Amy are desperate to find out what's happened to Rory, who's vanished too.

But something is waiting for them in the woods. Something that's been there for thousands of years. Something that is now waking up.

A thrilling, all-new adventure featuring the Doctor, Amy and Rory, as played by Matt Smith, Karen Gillan and Arthur Darvill in the spectacular hit series from BBC Television.

Available now from BBC Books:

DOCTOR WHO

Hunter's Moon

by Paul Finch

£6.99 ISBN 978 1 849 90236 6

Welcome to Leisure Platform 9 – a place where gamblers and villains rub shoulders with socialites and celebrities. Don't cheat at the games tables, and be careful who you beat. The prize for winning the wrong game is to take part in another, as Rory is about to discover – and the next game could be the death of him.

When Rory is kidnapped by the brutal crime lord Xord Krauzzen, the Doctor and Amy must go undercover to infiltrate the deadly contest being played out in the ruins of Gorgoror. But how long before Krauzzen realises the Doctor isn't a vicious mercenary and discovers what Amy is up to? It's only a matter of time.

And time is the one thing Rory and the other fugitives on Gorgoror don't have. They are the hunted in a game that can only end in death, and time for everyone is running out...

A thrilling, all-new adventure featuring the Doctor, Amy and Rory, as played by Matt Smith, Karen Gillan and Arthur Darvill in the spectacular hit series from BBC Television.

Available now from BBC Books:

by Steve Tribe and James Goss

£9.99 ISBN 978 1 849 90232 8

Exterminate!

The chilling battle cry of the Daleks has terrorised and terrified countless billions across thousands of worlds throughout time and space, from Skaro, Vulcan and Exxilon to the Medusa Cascade, Churchill's War Room and the opening of the Pandorica. This is the comprehensive history of the greatest enemies of the Doctor.

Learn about the Daleks' origins on the planet Skaro, how a Time Lord intervention altered the course of Dalek history, and how they emerged to wage war on Thals, Mechonoids, Movellans, Draconians and humans. With design artwork and photographs from five decades of *Doctor Who, The Dalek Handbook* also reveals the development of their iconic look and sound, and their enduring appeal in television, radio, books, comics and more.

Including the full story of the Daleks' centuries-long conflict with the one enemy they fear, the Doctor, *The Dalek Handbook* is the complete guide to the Daleks – in and out of their casings!

Available now from BBC Books:

DOCTOR WHO
Paradox Lost

by George Mann

£6.99 ISBN 978 1 849 90235 9

London 1910: An unsuspecting thief gets more than he bargained for when he breaks into a house in Kensington. He finds himself confronted by horrific, grey-skinned creatures that are waiting to devour his mind.

London 2789: An unimaginably ancient city. The remains of an android are dredged from the Thames. It's one of the latest models, only just developed. But it's been in the water for over a thousand years. And when the android is reactivated, it has a message – a warning that can only be delivered to a man named the Doctor.

The Doctor and his friends must solve a mystery that has spanned over a thousand years. Travelling backwards and forwards in time, they must unravel the threads of an ancient plot. If they fail, the deadly alien Squall will devour the world…

A thrilling, all-new adventure featuring the Doctor, Amy and Rory, as played by Matt Smith, Karen Gillan and Arthur Darvill in the spectacular hit series from BBC Television.

Available now from BBC Books:

DOCTOR WHO

Borrowed Time

by Naomi A. Alderman

£6.99 ISBN 978 1 849 90233 5

Andrew Brown never has enough time. No time to call his sister, no time to prepare for that important presentation at the bank where he works… The train's late, the lift jams, the all-important meeting's started by the time he arrives. Disaster.

If only he'd had just a little more time.

Time is the business of Mr Symington and Mr Blenkinsop. They'll lend Andrew Brown some time – at a very reasonable rate of interest. If he was in trouble before he borrowed time, things have just got a lot worse.

Detecting a problem, the Doctor, Amy and Rory go undercover at the bank. The Doctor's a respected expert, and Amy's his trusted advisor. Rory has a job in the post room. But they have to move fast to stop Symington and Blenkinsop before they cash in their investments. The Harvest is approaching.

A thrilling, all-new adventure featuring the Doctor, Amy and Rory, as played by Matt Smith, Karen Gillan and Arthur Darvill in the spectacular hit series from BBC Television.